BETTY CAVANNA
is the devoted owner of several cocker spaniels, which
are her favorite dogs. She divides her time between training them and writing about them — and does both extremely well. In addition to *The Black Spaniel Mystery,* she has also written another fine book about cockers: *Puppy Stakes.*

BETTY CAVANNA

THE
BLACK
SPANIEL
MYSTERY

ILLUSTRATED BY
GEORGETTE
DELATTRE

SCHOLASTIC BOOK SERVICES

Published by Scholastic Book Services, a division of Scholastic
Magazines, Inc., 33 West 42nd Street, New York 36, N. Y.

The Printing History of  THE BLACK SPANIEL MYSTERY

WESTMINSTER PRESS EDITION
PUBLISHED ....*May, 1945*

POCKET BOOK, JR. EDITION
PUBLISHED ....*February, 1951*

SCHOLASTIC BOOK EDITION
4th printing ....*August, 1961*

This SCHOLASTIC BOOK edition includes every word contained in the original, higher-priced edition. It is printed from plates made from completely reset, large, clear, easy-to-read type. It is published by arrangement with The Westminster Press and Pocket Books, Inc.

L

THE
BLACK
SPANIEL
MYSTERY

JEFF SAW THEM FIRST. THEY WERE JUST
two black specks in the distance, bobbing along in
the middle of the macadam road. He squinted against
the noon sun and watched them come closer, until he
could distinguish long ears jouncing rhythmically.
Then he nudged his twin.

"Look!"

Judy, her head turned the other direction in anticipation of the postman, leaned back on her elbows
in the warm grass and peered around the pillar of the
rural delivery box. They were trotting down the long
hill rapidly now, pink tongues lolling—two identical
spaniel puppies as shiny as wet black paint.

Judy's mouth opened in surprise. She laughed out

 loud and scrambled to her feet, dusting
the rear of her denim shorts with the
palm of one brown hand. "Aren't they
sweet, Jeff! Where d'you suppose they're
going?"

For there could be no doubt in the world that the puppies were headed somewhere. Their purposeful canter was carrying them along the country highway at a steady clip. Yet to Judy they seemed absurdly young to be off this way by themselves. Five or six months was her guess. Just small fry!

A truck rounded the bend at the top of the hill and Jeff's eyes leaped from the dogs to its spinning wheels and back to the dogs again. They were past the stone bridge now, past the entrance to the lane, almost abreast of the twins. "Wherever they're going, they're too young to be out alone, on a main highway. They'll get run down." Jeff whistled. "Come here, fellows!"

The pups didn't need coaxing. Judy crouched and held out her hand and one of the spaniels came to her at once, sniffed, wagged his stubby tail, then put both forepaws on her knees. Jeff held the other while the truck roared by, sinking his lean fingers into the deep, soft coat, rumpling the swaying ears. "They're pretty cute, all right! Big, gangly boys!" He cupped the muzzle of the dog he held with his free hand and turned the head up. "Where do you live, anyway?"

"Maybe they're lost! Maybe they could be ours!" Judy's brown eyes were shining. "They don't have collars, or identification tags, or anything!"

Jeff eyed his sister with patient male superiority. "Grow up, Judy. These pups are thoroughbreds."

Judy looked down at the dog in her lap. He was a friendly youngster, nipping and licking her hand alternately, squirming over on his back so that she could rub his belly. The dash of cold water on her impulsive hopes made her feel resentful. "How do you know?"

But before her brother could answer, the postman's jalopy rattled up, and Mr. Stretch was leaning out the window wheezing: "Well, well, well, where did you get the puppies? Twins for the twins, eh?"

Judy tried to smile politely, but Jeff ignored the feeble joke. "They're not ours," he said seriously. "We found them coming down the road—alone. Do you know who they might belong to?"

Mr. Stretch shook his head. "Lots of people round Wayne has cockers. Prob'ly they wandered off. Why don't you call the police?"

"The police?" Judy looked startled.

"Sure, the police," seconded Jeff. "Everybody calls the police when they lose a dog."

Mr. Stretch, meanwhile, was diving headfirst into the back of the car to sort out a handful of mail from among the assorted packages and envelopes which lay, in mysterious disarray, on the seat and floor. Judy stretched out her hand to receive the telephone bill, a motion-picture circular, and two letters addressed to Mrs. George Biggs Sutherland. "Is that all?" she asked.

"That's all." The postman's response was as automatic as Judy's question. He leaned out of the car window and pushed a package into the box marked "Rogers" and a single envelope into the one marked

"Matthews" which stood next to the Sutherland box. For just a second he paused with the Matthews letter in his hand. "There's a funny postmark," he chuckled. "Delaware, Ohio. Who ever heard of Delaware, Ohio?" Then he ground the old car into first gear and rattled off.

Jeff, looking after him, shook his head. "Isn't he an old busybody? I'll bet he reads every post card he leaves along his route."

"That was a good idea, though, about the pups," Judy put in. "Maybe we ought to call the police."

It wasn't difficult to persuade the dogs to follow them up the lane. Jeff ran ahead, calling: "Here, boy! Here, boy!" and Judy acted as guard, to see that they didn't stray back to the dangerous highway. By the time the four of them were halfway up the drive the pups were yelping and dancing, quite prepared to enjoy this new game.

From the door of the remodeled farmhouse Mrs. Sutherland watched the procession approach. Her eyes, full of amusement, glanced from the dogs to the twins, who were too absorbed in their companions to see her. Jeff was leaping from one side of the drive to the other with a black shadow at his heels, and Judy, who had stooped to caress the other puppy, was trying to disengage one of her beribboned pigtails from his insistent teeth.

Mrs. Sutherland laughed. Judy's absurd pigtails, a fad this summer with the high-school crowd, made her look like a little girl, in spite of the length of her slender brown legs. Sometimes she wished she could keep the twins young, could have the fun of the past ten years all over again, could go back to when they were five.

Judy had looked up at the sound of her laugh. "Hi, Mommy!" she called.

"Where on earth did you get those?" Mrs. Sutherland came forward along the old brick terrace, bordered by newly planted boxwood. Her hair, the same soft brown as Judy's, was twisted high on her head, and a few curling tendrils escaped to punctuate the surprised arch of her eyebrows.

Judy beat Jeff to an answer. "They came in the mail."

Both Jeff and his mother laughed, and the boy leaned down to gather one squirming black ball in his arms. He held the dog firmly and walked up to his mother. "It was nice of you to order two."

Mrs. Sutherland stroked the round head and smiled. "Where do they belong?"

"I don't know," Jeff said. "We found them coming down the highway. I'm going in and call the police."

But the police were as much in the dark as the twins about the ownership of the dogs. "Of course they haven't been lost long," said the voice of the sergeant on duty. "We'll probably have an inquiry before the day's out."

"And if they don't," commented Judy, "it's all right with me. I wish nobody'd claim them. Then we could adopt them legally. It would sort of make up for not being able to go to camp and the swimming pool being dry."

Mrs. Sutherland looked at her daughter in mild dismay. Judy was such a romanticist, always leaping to wonderful conclusions and having her daydreams smashed. She was so much less practical than Jeff, who was already saying logically: "Those are good pups. The owner'll turn up all right."

It was four o'clock in the afternoon, however, before a call came through from the police. As the intervening hours ticked away Judy's hopes rose. In her own mind she began to make plans, though she knew better than to mention them to Jeff, who was busy teaching the spaniels to retrieve. She had the dogs tentatively installed in a kennel of some elegance, which she and Jeff would build. She had them named, a dozen times, and she would try the names out on her lips, soundlessly, to see how they'd fit. Then, when the phone rang, and Jeff ran to answer it, she tried to tell herself that this wouldn't be the police—it would be for Mother. But of course, when Jeff came outside again, she knew.

"Who was it?" Her eyes were big with the question and her lips were turned down at the corners.

Jeff hated to tell her. "The police," he said. "The dogs belong to Mr. Artemus Gross. He'll be over after them."

"Oh!" Judy knew Artemus Gross by reputation.

He'd bought the old Lovell estate, up on the hill overlooking the valley road. Mother had told Dad about the huge stone entrance pillars, into which were chiseled the new name of the place, Gross Point, and Dad had smiled and shaken his head. "I suspect those pillars were chiseled in more ways than one," he'd said.

Jeff was trying to look at the pups, curled up together by the terrace steps sound asleep, with a disinterest he didn't feel. He wished that Artemus Gross weren't the owner. He wished they belonged to some child who would play with them and love them. But aloud he said, "I think I heard somewhere that Mr. Gross was breeding dogs."

"Why?" asked Judy. "He's awfully rich, isn't he?"

Jeff shrugged. "Sometimes rich people breed dogs—just for fun."

Judy interrupted, suddenly alert as a thought struck her. "Maybe we could buy them!"

Her brother shook his head. "Not a chance. Not this summer. If there isn't enough money for camp there isn't enough to buy two thoroughbred cockers. They cost a lot."

"How much?" Judy wanted to know.

"I don't know. A lot."

Judy looked at the sleeping puppies speculatively. "Fifty dollars?"

But Jeff didn't answer. His head was turned toward the road, where he could hear a car coming down the hill. Could this be Mr. Gross so soon? Then he was relieved to hear the screeching brakes which identified the bus from town stopping at the end of the lane. He crouched down to peer through the screen of trees that sheltered the Sutherlands' garden. "It's just Lynn Matthews," he said.

The girl who climbed down from the bus had her arms full of bundles, which she adjusted to a more comfortable carrying position before she started slow-  ly up the lane. It was a long, rutted road which led through what had once been a cow pasture to the house on the top of the hill where she lived with her father. It went past the Sutherland place, past the Rogers' house, and on up and up until it stopped at a tumble-down gate beyond which was the Matthews' chicken yard.

Jeff, now sprawled on the grass, watched her come up the lane idly. She was a very slender girl—almost thin—and she had fair, straight hair and a serious face with big gray eyes. Her father, a gardener who took work by the day, had the same eyes, except that his looked tired where Lynn's looked apologetic. She was extremely shy, and Jeff, accustomed to Judy's enthusiastic high spirits, always felt rather sorry for her. He called to her now, wondering whether he should offer to help her up the hill with her parcels. "Hi, Lynn."

The puppies, awakened by the note of his voice, looked up with a start, and then, hearing the crunch of footsteps on the gravel, raced across the lawn toward the sound, barking half in greeting and half in warning as spaniels do.

"Hello," Lynn started to say, ducking her head a little to look under the leafy, low-hanging branch of a dogwood. Then she heard and saw the dogs! "Why! Why, for ... My puppies! How did they get out?" She let her packages slide out of her arms to the edge of the lawn and came forward hurriedly, to crouch down on the grass as the spaniels gamboled around her, wagging their tails and climbing up in excitement to lick her face.

"*Your* puppies?" Jeff's voice, puzzled and disbelieving, stifled a laugh.

"*Your* puppies?" Judy got to her feet from the deck chair where she had been lying and took a couple of uncertain steps forward.

The surprise in the twins' voices was unmistakable. Lynn pushed the dogs gently from her and got to her feet. "Why, yes," she said. "I can't imagine how they got out of their pen."

"I didn't know you had any puppies." Judy blurted the words out, glancing from the dogs, who had abandoned Lynn to nip at each other's ears, to the girl. She knew Lynn better than Jeff did, because the gardener's daughter was in her home room at school, and on the couple of occasions when she'd climbed the long hill to the Matthews' house to consult her classmate on some schoolwork, she'd never seen any animals except chickens around the yard.

"I haven't had them long," Lynn stammered. "Just a couple of weeks." She dropped her eyes in what looked to Jeff like embarrassment and whistled softly. "Here, Shadow! Here, Sambo!" The pups stopped playing and ran toward her in delight. She rumpled their ears and smiled, then stood up and faced the twins as the dogs started to tumble each other over again. "Where did you find them?"

"They were coming down the highway," Judy started to explain, waving her hand toward the road, but Jeff interrupted her.

"Look here, Lynn," he said quickly. "We called the police before lunch to see if we could find the owner, and the police just called back to say they belong at Gross Point. Mr. Gross is supposed to be on his way down here now."

Judy tried to lighten this news with a laugh. "This is a fine mix-up!"

But Lynn might not have heard her. She was looking at Jeff. "There must be some mistake. They're my puppies. You can see they knew me at once!"

"Then I ought to call the police back and head Mr. Gross off." Jeff, impressed by Lynn's sincerity, started for the house. The eyes of both girls followed him. Judy's were puzzled, Lynn's wondering and slightly concerned. "I'm sorry . . ." she murmured hesitantly.

"Oh, don't worry!" Judy tried to put Lynn at ease by being breezy. "Mr. Gross probably lost two other dogs. Anyway," she went on, "these pups of yours didn't look lost. They looked as if they were going somewhere." Then she stopped abruptly as a thought occurred to her. The dogs hadn't been coming from the Matthews' and they hadn't been headed toward the Matthews'. If they had, they would have turned in at the lane. They'd been coming down the road when Jeff first saw them, and they'd already passed the lane when he called them over to him. Strange!

She might have mentioned this impulsively to Lynn if Jeff, just then, hadn't banged out of the door and jumped from the terrace to the lawn. "It was too late to catch Mr. Gross," he called. Then he added, as he came closer, "But Sergeant Cudahy—I think that's his name—says he'll ride out in a little while and try to get this tangle straightened out."

"But there isn't any tangle," Lynn said, shaking her head gently and spreading her hands. She was looking directly at Jeff, and the boy thought that when she forgot to be shy she was almost pretty. Not pretty in a vivacious, dashing sort of way, like Judy and his mother, but soft and quiet and cool-looking, like the creek below the house.

"I know," he nodded, "but the cops probably think we're just a gang of kids."

"Think?" Judy could never quite accept the fact that she was almost grown up, not unless she sat down and considered it very seriously. But the way she said, "Think?" made both Lynn and Jeff laugh, and they were still smiling when a rackety black coupé bustled up the drive.

"That's never Mr. Gross," said Jeff. "The sergeant must have hurried."

The sergeant was still hurrying when he slammed the door of his car and came down the brick walk to the garden. "Hello. Hello. Hello," he said with professional good nature. "Now what's this mix-up all about?" He looked from the dogs to the twins and finally to Lynn, where his eyes rested.

"There isn't any mix-up, sir," explained Lynn in her shy voice. "It's just that Judy and Jeff Sutherland happened to find my puppies. They must have got out of their pen."

"But Mr. Artemus Gross says they're his dogs."

Lynn shook her head. "He hasn't seen them. He'll know when he sees them."

"Where is he?" asked Sergeant Cudahy. "He ought to be here by now."

Almost as he spoke a long gray car pulled into the drive, sliding to a stop where the brick walk cut through the hedge. The man who climbed from the back seat was massive and far from agile. Through the screen of leaves Judy caught a glimpse of a thick neck which bulged uncomfortably over the collar of a neat striped shirt. Dull reddish hair, tinged with gray, was plastered against his forehead, and he had a heavy mottling of freckles over his nose. He grunted as he eased himself out of the car, then, looking through the hedge, he saw the policeman with the dogs and the children and came directly toward them.

The ragged wisps of eyebrows that jutted above his bright eyes moved upward as Mr. Gross spoke to the sergeant. "Well, I'm certainly glad you caught up with them, officer!" he said with a smile of relief. "Those pups mean a lot to me! My kennelman must have left the door off the latch. Carelessness. Inexcusable carelessness!"

Judy had to admit that the man's deep voice carried conviction. She was, as a matter of fact, so absorbed in studying Mr. Gross himself that it was several seconds before she realized the import of what he said. Hastily, then, she glanced toward Lynn Matthews. A slow flush, whether of anger or embarrassment Judy couldn't tell, was creeping up the girl's face. She was breathing heavily, as though she had been running, and her eyes were glued to Mr. Gross, who had given her no more than a cursory glance.

The big man was bending down now, snapping his fingers. "Here, pups!" The words rapped out with executive command and the puppies stopped playing and ran over to Mr. Gross at once, tails wagging and red tongues lolling. They may have made less fuss over the newcomer than they had over Lynn, but then Mr. Gross wasn't sitting invitingly on the grass. "Know their master all right," said the owner of Gross Point.

The sergeant, Judy, and Jeff were all looking at Artemus Gross. Mr. Gross was looking down at the pups, who were leaping against his knees. With a pudgy but neatly manicured hand he was making vague patting motions in the air, now hitting a puppy's head, now missing it. For a moment nobody said a word. Then Lynn unexpectedly streaked across the lawn to gather the pups in her arms. Her eyes filled with tears and she turned frantically to Sergeant Cudahy, who looked baffled and uncertain.

"But, officer," she cried. "These aren't his dogs! They're mine!"

2

"THEY'RE MINE!" Lynn repeated the words with more defiance than Judy had ever seen her display. She clutched the wriggling puppies to her and looked directly at Sergeant Cudahy, ignoring Mr. Gross.

The officer looked from Lynn to Mr. Gross, who was standing by with a great show of patience, then back to the excited girl again, and said, as though he were humoring a child: "Come, come. There can't be two sets of black cockers roaming the roads around Wayne."

The twins could tell, from the uncertainty of the policeman's voice, that Lynn's outburst had puzzled him. He was a conscientious man, with receding fair hair that stood in a cockscomb above his anxious forehead. He seemed to be enjoying this scrap so little that Judy couldn't help wondering why he'd ever become an officer of the law at all. But somehow not Cudahy's tone of voice but the words he spoke made Lynn look hysterical and foolish. The effect was heightened by the fact that Mr. Gross threw his head back and laughed loudly.

Judy and Jeff squirmed in embarrassment. The situation was getting beyond them. They were relieved that their mother appeared on the terrace just then and came on down the steps to the garden. Jeff introduced her to Sergeant Cudahy and Mr. Gross, and she spoke pleasantly to Lynn, whom she knew. But she was on her way down the road to call on some friends and she left them at once, without being aware of the turn of events. Jeff opened his mouth to tell her, then thought better of it. This was his and Judy's problem.

To Mr. Gross, however, it seemed no problem at all. As soon as Mrs. Sutherland had walked away he turned to Sergeant Cudahy, and in a cool, businesslike manner proceeded to override Lynn's claim to the pups. His voice was steady and convincing, his shoe-button eyes level. Judy looked from Gross to Lynn in dismay. It didn't seem possible that this big, hearty man could be wrong, yet Lynn's sincerity was obvious. The girl, who was standing by fighting back tears, with both hands now clenched in front of her, really *believed* the dogs to be hers.

Finally Mr. Gross turned to Lynn and said, unctuously, "What's your name, young lady?"

"Lynn Matthews."

Gross raised his eyebrows. "So!" Then he added, "You're Mike Matthews' girl, aren't you?" The condescension in his voice was obvious.

Lynn, apparently not trusting herself to speak, nodded.

The man turned to Sergeant Cudahy and said, in an undertone that nevertheless carried both to the twins and to Lynn: "Father used to work on my place. Shiftless sort of chap."

Lynn, now even closer to tears, surprised Judy and Jeff by stamping her foot. "He is not!" she denied hotly. "And these *are* my dogs!"

Once more the policeman's attention veered to Lynn, and he became more confused than ever. In the argument which followed he did his best to get at the root of the misunderstanding while Gross became impatient and Lynn almost hysterical. It was inevitable, even though Sergeant Cudahy tried to be fair-minded, that he should favor Mr. Gross's claim. The man pointed out that the black puppies were unusually fine, part of a litter from which he expected to get some first-rate specimens for showing. He added, with weary but determined affability, that the litter was of course registered, even though the individual dogs did not yet have their papers, and that the sergeant was welcome to see the document if he needed any further proof of his word.

It all sounded very reasonable, even to Jeff and Judy. It made Lynn's insistence that Shadow and Sambo knew their names and would come to her when she called seem juvenile and unsubstantial.

"They'll come to anybody, miss," the cop pointed

out. "They'll even come to me, and I could call 'em Rex and Rover, for all they'd care." He proved his point by doing so, and the pups came over at once, happy as could be at the attention.

The litter registration argument seemed to clinch the matter in Sergeant Cudahy's mind, and he was ready to award the dogs to Gross and be off about his business, but Jeff, worried by Lynn's increasing distress, wanted to be entirely fair.

"Look, sergeant," he said. "My sister and I found the dogs. We didn't know we were going to get into such a mix-up, but now that we have I'd like the decision to be square. Couldn't you ride over to Gross Point and take a look at that paper, just to be sure?"

For an instant Judy thought that Gross's eyes narrowed, as though he resented his authority being questioned, but when Cudahy, decently enough, fell in with Jeff's suggestion, he shrugged his shoulders and said: "All right. Come on." He then adopted an attitude of patient willingness to go to any lengths to humor the twins, because they had been instrumental in the dogs' return.

It was a short trip to the big house—just half a mile —and Lynn, while she waited with the Sutherlands for the return of the Gross car, said very little. She sat down on the grass where she had been standing, and when the spaniels came to her she clutched them close, stroking their ears, talking to them in a broken mur-

mur, as though at any minute they would surely be snatched away.

All the fight now seemed to have left her. She was convinced that Mr. Gross would get the puppies. And it was her very resignation that confused and worried Jeff. Was it because Lynn was poor and Mr. Gross was wealthy? Why was she giving up the scrap? Could the dogs be really hers? Finally he put a question to her.

"If they're your dogs, where did you get them?"

But Lynn, looking down, shook her head. "I can't tell."

Judy glanced at her twin in a way that said, "Curiouser and curiouser." Then she turned to Lynn and forthrightly burst out: "Can't tell? Why not?"

Lynn's answer was very faint but very determined. "I just can't, that's all."

Instead of putting Judy off, Lynn's insistence intrigued her. She took delight in anything mysterious, and in her own mind she was as adventurous as her favorite heroine, Sue Barton, if only opportunity would knock. When her father had bought the old farmhouse to remodel, four years before, she'd had high hopes, and Jeff had teased her when she confessed her disappointment that there were no hidden staircases or buried gold behind the rotting plaster walls. Now it was as neat and prim as a polished Indian-head penny with the surfaces rubbed down by age, and the chance that Judy would find a lost will, a hidden fortune, or even a broken locket about the place was slim indeed. Still, it was fun to lose herself in a mystery story, and even though she realized regretfully that things of which she read never happened in real life, she could still hope. Kneeling down beside Lynn, Judy rocked back on her heels. Sue Barton, now, would ask some leading questions.

But she couldn't think of any questions that really helped. Lynn admitted, willingly enough, that she had no papers—whatever they were—for the dogs, no way of proving her ownership, only her word and the word of her father, which Artemus Gross had managed to convey would be of dubious value. "Anyway," said Lynn, "Daddy won't be home till tonight."

Jeff was getting more restless and uncomfortable by the minute and he kept trying to call Judy off. "Let Lynn alone," he said finally. "She's said everything there is to say." He was beginning to wish he'd never found the puppies at all and got involved in this scrap. Though he was inclined to believe Lynn's claim, it did seem unlikely that she would come by two highly bred cockers, and the weight of evidence was certainly all on Mr. Gross's side. He rubbed his cropped brown hair with his hand and frowned, hoping that the two men would hurry back and that there would be an end to it.

When Mr. Gross did return, with Cudahy at his heels, he was smiling confidently, and his manner was more bustling and impressive than ever. The sergeant explained at once that the papers were in order, and that he was now convinced that the puppies had wandered off from the Gross Point kennels. Lynn stood in the background, hands clenched behind her back, but she hadn't a word to say, even when Mr. Gross's chauffeur lifted the puppies into the big car.

Mr. Gross, in saying his goodbyes, was even inclined to turn a benign smile on Lynn, though it was barbed with a parting thrust. "*If* you ever owned two black cockers, you'll probably find them scratching at your back door when you get home."

He climbed into the car with a grunt. The chauffeur slammed the door, and the automobile moved off to make the circle by the garage. Lynn's chin trembled as she stood with the twins watching the car for a moment. Then she walked back to the lawn where her neglected packages lay. The turn was made, and the long gray automobile started to roll down the drive, when Mr. Gross leaned forward and tapped his chauffeur's shoulder and again the machine pulled to a stop.

Grunting, Mr. Gross climbed out, and walking back across the lawn to the twins, extracted a bill from a wallet which he took out of his pocket. "I forgot. I'd like to pay you for your trouble," he said.

Judy, intensely embarrassed, was glad she had a twin who was a boy. It was Jeff who had to refuse the money, and he did it abruptly, leaving Mr. Gross in little doubt that this belated gesture was an insult.

Shrugging, the fat man crushed the bill in his hand and turned away.

"Golly, did you see the size of that greenback!" Jeff muttered to Judy as the car at last rolled down the drive. "It was a twenty! That old geezer must set some store by those dogs!"

But Judy's eyes were following Lynn, now quite overcome, who had already left the Sutherland driveway and started off up the rutted lane toward her home. "We ought to walk up with her," Judy suggested warmheartedly. "I don't know who the pups really belong to, but she's certainly plenty upset."

"O.K.," Jeff consented, thinking of the heavy packages Lynn was lugging, and with his twin he hurried up the hill.

Lynn, if she heard them coming, didn't turn around, and when Jeff and Judy caught up with her they realized that she was really crying. It was hard to know what to say or do. Jeff took one of the bags full of groceries, but Lynn shook her head when Judy tried to take the other. "I can carry it," she said.

"Look," Judy suggested, trying to comfort her, since she couldn't be of any physical aid, "maybe Mr. Gross was right. Maybe your own dogs are home by now." But Lynn only shook her head again, and to Jeff's discomfiture cried all the harder. For a hundred yards or so they walked along in silence.

Judy was very much disturbed. She didn't know Lynn very well, but at school she'd always seemed a quiet, reserved girl, not the crying type. Keeping house for her father as she did, she never had much time for sports, or dramatics, or any other extracurricular activities. Besides, Judy suspected, the extra money for a season ticket for football games and such was hard for Lynn to come by. She was a fair student, not brilliant, but able to think on her feet if the occasion demanded it, and the fact that she had gone so completely to pieces over this matter of a couple of puppies seemed out of character to the extreme. For the life of her, Judy couldn't think of anything else to say.

Jeff, walking a little behind the two girls, was wishing women wouldn't always cry, just on general principles. He couldn't see how tears could possibly help. They only made him mad. He'd been inclined to like Lynn, awhile before, to believe her and sympathize with her, but now she only irritated him. Why in the dickens couldn't she stop bawling? Jiminy Christmas! Angrily he kicked at a stone with his heel and sent it plunging down the hill.

Judy turned around and frowned at him and Jeff twisted his mouth up on one side and shook his head. Each understood completely what the other meant.

They were halfway up the hill now, and the path had turned to the left, so that the valley lay stretched below them, and white clapboard and gray-stone houses peeked out from their perches among the green trees on the opposite hills. Beyond them the sun was dropping, so that the fields at their feet lost their brilliance, and looked parched and dry. Immediately below was the roof of the Rogers' house, and farther down the sloping green roof of their own home, while far off, on the other range, the towers of Gross Point caught a final glint of sunlight. By now, Judy was thinking, Shadow and Sambo are home. She couldn't help calling the dogs by Lynn's names for them. They fitted them, somehow. She wondered how they liked living in a kennel. If she were a dog, she decided, she'd rather live in a home—a home where you could climb on the furniture, and lie on people's laps, and have your tummy rubbed. . . .

"Say, Lynn!" Jeff's sharp voice, immediately behind her, made Judy jump. "Didn't you say you'd been in to town? When were you home last? How did you even know your dogs had got away?"

Lynn stopped crying and turned to look at Jeff curiously—as though, Judy said later, she considered him not quite bright. "I haven't been home since breakfast," she said, "but the minute I saw the pups on your lawn I knew they were Shadow and Sambo. What are you talking about?"

Judy giggled. She couldn't help it. Her brown eyes twinkled, and she bit her lower lip to hide a grin. As an amateur detective Jeff would make a good brick-layer, and when she had an opportunity she intended to tell him so. At the moment, however, she was out of breath. Lynn, used to the climb, had set a swift pace, and the three reached the top of the rocky hill and came within sight of the Matthews' yard. It was a dismal enough affair, seen through the break in the trees, for all of Lynn's efforts at tidiness. Chickens pecked here and there among the bright flowers that bordered the sagging fence. Beyond the blooms the house looked weather-beaten and run down.

"The dog pen," offered Lynn, "is over on the other side, out of the wind. Daddy built it."

As she finished speaking there was a bark, then an-other, then a series of bright, quick yelps. Judy looked at Lynn, and so did Jeff, while Lynn's mouth dropped in astonishment. Then Judy yelled, "Hey!" and broke into a sprint. Jeff and Lynn dumped their packages on the ground and followed. By the time the latter two had rounded the corner of the house Judy was on her knees in front of a homemade run, and against the wire were jumping and pawing two black spaniel puppies, four or five months old, as alike as two peas in a pod.

"Look!" Relief flooded Judy's face as she turned to Lynn and Jeff.

"Say!" Jeff grinned, but Lynn walked forward slowly to stare down at the excited dogs in disbelief.

"How did they ever get back here? Was Mr. Gross fooling?" Judy had a dozen questions that cried to be answered.

But before she could say a word Lynn turned to her and cried, wildly: "Can't you see? These aren't our dogs!"

3

"Aren't—your—dogs?"

Judy spoke each word separately, as though she were dreaming. Jeff, equally incredulous, was also getting tired of this game. "You must be mistaken, Lynn," he said sharply. "Just look at them!"

Lynn looked, but she shook her head. She even went over and picked one of the puppies up in her arms, stroking its head and back and looking into its eyes. She didn't say a word, but Judy was voluble.

"Oh, but they *must* be yours, Lynn! You're just overwrought. See, they're just delighted to see you. They must know you. They're making such a fuss!"

Lynn, now completely dry-eyed, shook her head again. "A cocker puppy will make a fuss over anybody," she said flatly. "You saw that this afternoon." Gently she put the dog back in the pen. "They're sweet babies, but they're simply not ours."

Jeff sighed heavily. He went closer to the pen and crouched down, putting out his hand, and as Lynn had predicted the pups made just as much of a play for the boy's attention as they had for the girl's. Judy, reduced for a moment to speechlessness, looked closely at the dogs too. Each was coal black, without a wisp of white anywhere, and each had the same full, round eyes and long curly ears. But were they quite as curly as Shadow's and Sambo's? Were the coats quite as thick? Could the heads be a little flatter? Or was she just imagining these things because of Lynn's insistence? She simply couldn't tell.

"What makes you so sure they're not yours, Lynn?" Jeff was saying. "They look like the same pups to me."

Lynn stared at Jeff. "Oh, no!" she cried. "They don't look a bit alike really! Can't you tell?" She picked one pup up by the scruff of the neck and set him on the ground before her. "Look! They haven't the feathers. They aren't so well knit. Their ears are set too high." Her slender fingers traced the faults of which she spoke. She seemed very sure of her facts.

Judy murmured, "I was thinking there was something about the ears," but Jeff said, honestly, "Neither of us knows a thing about spaniels, but to me those pups look as much like the ones Judy and I picked up as peas in a pod."

"Don't you think you *could* be mistaken?" said Judy hopefully. "How long had you had your puppies?"

"Only about two weeks."

"Well, then . . ."

"But I've fed them three times a day. I've played

with them. I've combed them. I couldn't *not* know my own pups."

Judy said dubiously, "But when they look so much alike . . ."

Lynn couldn't help seeing that the twins were uncertain of her judgment. "An average person might be fooled," she was willing to admit, "though I'm as certain of what I'm saying as I've ever been of anything in my life. But a breeder wouldn't be fooled."

"Mr. Gross is a breeder," Jeff reminded her.

"A gentleman breeder," Lynn said, as though this dismissed him. "He has a kennelman to do the work. Dad will know instantly, just as I did. As soon as he comes home he'll know!"

It was obvious that Lynn was inconsolable, and that the discussion was getting them all nowhere. This had been an afternoon full of talking and dispute, and Judy's head was beginning to spin. "Well, I can't really see what difference it makes, anyway," she said in a parting gesture of comfort. "You have two dogs; Mr. Gross has two dogs. They're all of them cute as pie. Toss 'em up in a basket and what does it matter which comes out?" She smiled sweetly.

It was Lynn's turn to look incredulous. "Oh, but you don't understand!" she started. Then she must have thought better of what she was going to say, because she stopped abruptly. "Well, all this certainly isn't your funeral," she said in a different tone, attempting a smile. "You've been awfully nice, and I *do* thank you!" She seemed to be anxious to remember her manners, and walked with them both to the gate, shooing the chickens and thanking them again for their help. But all the time the twins felt that she was making a great effort to be natural, and that she was really worried almost to distraction. They couldn't help feeling sorry for her. She seemed so concerned.

Once out of her sight, however, and away from the persuasive sincerity of her voice, the whole situation began to appear ridiculous to Jeff. "Such a lot of fuss about a couple of pups!" he growled, his eyebrows pulled down over his deep-set brown eyes in a way that reminded Judy of her father. "I wish we'd let them go on walking—wherever they were going."

Wherever they were going. Judy stopped dead. "I just thought of something—something that dawned on me this afternoon!" She picked up a stick from the high grass at the side of the lane and began prodding the road in front of her. "You *did* think those pups looked as though they were going somewhere, didn't you?"

"Uh-huh. Matter of fact we both said something about it."

Judy's eyes began to sparkle. "Well, they weren't headed toward Gross Point. They were going in the opposite direction."

"Mm-mph." Jeff grunted, looking out of the side of his eyes at Judy with something close to respect.

"As a matter of fact," his sister went on, "they

weren't headed toward the Matthews' either. If they had been, they'd have turned in at the lane."

Jeff looked disheartened. "So what does that prove?"

"Prove?" Judy felt deflated. "Well, they did look as if they were going somewhere," she argued grumpily. "And it was just about lunchtime. You'd think they'd be old enough to know how to turn around and go home."

Jeff shrugged, and Judy, with the close affinity of one twin for the other, knew that she had failed to come through with something he'd hoped would be important. Still, she had a hazy notion that it did prove something, though what she couldn't quite grasp. What she had managed to do was to flick Jeff's interest to the questioning point again.

"Look," he said, "you know Lynn better than I do. Think back—as far back as you can remember Lynn. D'you ever recall her telling a lie?"

"Of course not!" Judy protested. "She's not the type that tells fibs."

"I wouldn't think so, but sometimes the quiet ones fool you." Jeff shook himself like a dog after a bath. "This whole thing's crazy—loony crazy. Where would Lynn Matthews get two really good cockers, anyway? No breeder's going to let two pups go to his gardener, even supposing Mr. Matthews were working for a breeder."

"Which he isn't. He's working by the day, I think."

"All right. But to give Lynn the benefit of the doubt, just suppose she did get them as a gift. Then why in the dickens won't she tell who gave 'em to her?" Jeff sounded disgusted.

"She didn't say, 'I won't tell,'" denied Judy, leaping to the defense of her sex. "She said, 'I can't tell.'"

But Jeff only groaned and pretended to stagger. "Women!" he wailed aloud, holding his head with both hands.

Through his groan cut the insistent ring of an old dinner bell which Mrs. Sutherland had picked up at an auction and which she now used to call her children or her husband to meals when they strayed far from home. Jeff put both hands to his mouth, megaphone fashion. "Coming!" he shouted and, with Judy, started to run.

Jeff reached the kitchen door first, and held it open for Judy, a habit so newly acquired that it always surprised her. Judy, forgetting to say thanks, burst pellmell into the kitchen, anxious to begin at once on the story of their afternoon. "Mommy, the most amazing thing . . ."

"Keep it for dinner!" Jeff stopped her. "Then we won't have to go through it twice."

Mrs. Sutherland shot her son an appreciative glance. In all the years of her marriage she had never found a way to avoid the last-minute flurry before dinner. Water to pour, milk for the twins, butter on the butter plates, the hot biscuits to take out of the oven, vegetables to drain, the chops to put on a platter. Her mind danced from one to another domestic job. "Judy, could you . . ." Then she glanced at her daughter. "Good heavens," she interrupted herself, "go wash your face and hands."

It was her husband who eventually helped her, moving in and out of the kitchen with the same easy concentration that Jeff had inherited. He talked to her at the same time, about something amusing that had happened in the office, and his deep voice had a comfortable rumble which was very soothing, though Sheila Sutherland heard little that he said. Still, she laughed in the right places, or when her husband paused to chuckle, and as on every other evening, the family was finally assembled and the water and milk were poured and the hot biscuits, snuggled warmly in the folds of a white linen napkin, were starting to go their rounds.

Judy, her face scrubbed and shining, without benefit of the dusting of powder she used for occasions not strictly "family," took two. "Now can I?" she said.

Mrs. Sutherland passed the biscuits on to Jeff and started to serve the vegetables. "May you what?"

"O Mommy, you *know!*" To Judy her mother always seemed absurdly absent-minded. "Tell you about this afternoon."

"There isn't so much to tell," Jeff said glumly with his mouth full of hot biscuit. "It's all pretty senseless."

"That's just why it's interesting!" Judy insisted,

squirming forward and leaning both elbows on the table, the food before her still untouched. "First we found the dogs . . ."

"What dogs?" asked Mr. Sutherland.

"Eat your dinner, dear," said her mother.

But in spite of interruptions, Judy managed to get her story launched. Once started, she knew she could get her parents' attention. She could dramatize the situation, and draw the characters of Cudahy and Mr. Gross, with words like swift brush strokes. Sometimes she was tempted to exaggerate, but if she went too far she knew Jeff would be bound to stop her. It was only in trying to describe Lynn that she had trouble. Lynn seemed to Judy so meek, so lacking in color, that her outburst of the afternoon didn't fit in.

Her father, apparently, grasped at this discrepancy. He shook his head when Judy had finished. "Sounds to me like a tempest in a teapot," he murmured, leaning back in his chair. "Artemus Gross has never had a spotless reputation in business, but I can hardly see him stooping to dishonest dealings where a couple of pups are concerned." He chuckled at the very thought.

"Lynn Matthews is very young, and they live up there all alone," put in his wife. "If it were anything serious, dear, but it isn't . . ."

"It's serious to Lynn," said Jeff.

Mr. Sutherland shook his head. "I'm afraid you must accept the fact that Lynn got overexcited and is mistaken. Probably tomorrow morning she'll come down and tell you her father says her own pups were safe in the pen all the time. It's a coincidence that there should be two sets of black cockers, but as far as I can see that's the only mysterious element involved. And now," he added, "may I have my dessert? What is it?"

"Cake."

The eyebrows of both men in the family rose in pleasure. Judy cleared the table and Jeff, with a system they had developed, rinsed and stacked dishes in the kitchen. By the time they had returned the conversation was in adult hands, and the twins recognized from experience that their innings were over, for this meal at least.

After dinner Mr. and Mrs. Sutherland left almost at once to keep a bridge date, and Judy and Jeff wandered down the hill to take another look at the swimming pool, which a long summer drought had reduced to uselessness. It had been made by damming a creek that flowed down the hill through the woods, crossing the Matthews' land and then dropping past the Rogers' and the Sutherlands'. It was a rough sort of pool, not large, but usually deep enough. Together Mr. Rogers and Mr. Sutherland had built a diving board, and both families shared its advantages in hot weather.

"If we don't have some rain soon," Jeff said disconsolately, "we won't have any swimming all summer."

They both looked up at the darkening sky, clear as a silver bell. Judy walked out on the diving board and sat down on the end, swinging her legs and wriggling her heels in and out of her loafers. "It's a nice night," she said, unperturbed.

At intervals they could hear cars pass on the highway. Then a truck, changing gears laboriously, struggled up the hill. Crickets chirped with loud insistence and a frog plopped into the pool. "The thing I didn't like," barked Jeff suddenly, "was that guy offering me money. Who does he think he is, anyway? If he didn't have a nerve!"

The explosion was so unexpected that Judy laughed aloud. She had a hearty laugh, like her dad's, not the clear, tinkling, feminine laugh that people expected because she looked so much like her mother.

"Well, I don't care!" Jeff persisted. "That made me sore. You'd think he could see we weren't that kind. I didn't like the guy from the minute I saw him."

"He was pretty overbearing," Judy admitted lazily, looking up at the high-riding sliver of a new moon.

"He liked himself too darned well!" growled Jeff, less able to cope with adjectives and adverbs than Judy, who read three books to his one.

"With twenty dollars, though," said Judy with a yawn and a giggle, "you could've done a lot. You could've . . ."

"Judy Sutherland, why you grasping little so-and-so!" Coming up behind her on the diving board, Jeff pushed her shoulders with a quick jerk, so that she had to hang on tight with both hands to avoid falling in.

"Hey! Look out!" Judy swung around, and grinned at the disapproval on Jeff's face. "I didn't mean I'd have taken it."

Jeff looked down at her quizzically. "Well, I certainly hope not!" he said indignantly, then added: "But I'm not so sure. You've got a mercenary streak."

"But I *earn* my money," Judy reminded him.

"If you call 'baby sitting' work. All you do is go sit on somebody's davenport while the family goes to the movies."

"I lie," said Judy. "I take a book and lie down."

Jeff shook his head in disgust. "What would you do if the baby woke up and cried?"

"They never do, but if one did, and saying, 'Kutsy-kutsy-coo,' didn't work, I guess I'd call up Mother."

Jeff snorted, but Judy retaliated with, "Well, what would you do if the lawn mower broke while you were cutting the Davidsons' grass?" This was Jeff's one effort at summer occupation, and it took him a morning each week.

"I'd try to fix it."

"And if you couldn't?"

"I'd . . . Oh, shut up, Judy! You're an itch. Come on. Let's go up to the house."

The twins had rooms on either side of their own bath at the back of the house, which had been remodeled with the Sutherlands' special needs in mind.

Two rooms had been thrown together to make their parents' big bedroom at the front, and an old closet had been turned into a second bathroom. Judy went upstairs at once and got into pajamas. Reading in bed was her favorite indoor sport, but it seemed a stupid occupation to Jeff, who went down to his workshop in the basement to tinker with the radio which he had taken apart and put together again with absorbing interest at regular intervals over the past year.

When Jeff came upstairs he was sleepy. While he had been working he'd thought idly of the affair of the lost puppies. Lynn's first reaction on seeing the dogs had been so forthright and honest that he'd sided with her at once. Yet later developments had baffled him. Whether he liked Mr. Gross or not, Jeff had to admit that all the conclusive evidence was on his side. The puppies certainly must have been his. It was a funny thing, Jeff decided, but no more than a funny thing. He was going to put the whole business out of his mind before he got in a stew about it.

But while Jeff had reasoned logically and calmly as he used his hands, which was a process that always soothed and rested him, Judy, involved in a mystery story, was stimulated. She called to her twin when she heard him brushing his teeth.

"Jeff!"

"Huh?" His grunt meant, "Let me alone."

"Come here."

Jeff walked into Judy's room to see her sitting up in

bed, very alert, her book abandoned by her side and her slim arms hugging her seersucker-clad knees. "What d'you want?"

"I was just reading this story about two kidnaped babies found in an abandoned rowboat, and I was thinking that if the puppies had been babies, wouldn't it make a swell plot!"

"But they're not," Jeff replied irritably.

"But if they were!"

"In real life they never are—only in books. For goodness' sakes, Judy, forget it!"

By the middle of the next morning Judy had just about decided to follow Jeff's advice. In an old pair of dungarees and a man's work shirt she was helping her brother to oil her bike when Lynn burst into the garage. Though the girl was breathless from running downhill she couldn't wait to tell the twins that she'd thought of a sure way to identify her dogs.

"They haven't any dewclaws," she gasped. "Shadow and Sambo haven't any dewclaws."

"Any what?" asked Judy.

"Any dewclaws. Any fifth toes on their forelegs."

"Any fifth toes? What are you talking about?" It sounded to Jeff as though maybe this girl were balmy after all.

Lynn leaned against the side of the trash barrel and tried to explain. "Cocker spaniels have their tails cut, you know, when they're very young—four or five days old."

Judy didn't know, but she tried to look intelligent. "Yes?"

Jeff, in his turn, looked completely puzzled. What in thunder did fifth toes have to do with tails, and what were dewclaws anyway? Claws didn't sound like toes to him. He watched Lynn very closely and tried to detect some sign of mental trouble. He felt very confused.

"Well, lots of times when he cuts a puppy's tail the vet takes off the fifth toe too. It isn't any good, you see —it's like an appendix, just sort of a nuisance—and, besides, if a dog's allowed to run in the fields, he's apt to tear it."

"Tear what, his appendix?" Judy, by now, was completely at sea.

"No," said Lynn patiently, "his dewclaw."

"You mean 'them,' don't you?" asked Jeff.

"All right, them." She looked at the boy. "D'you think I'd better go back and begin over?"

"No. Go on." Judy spoke impatiently.

"Well, my pups didn't have any dewclaws, and those two that are up in the pen now *have*."

The twins looked at each other. This was interesting. "You're certain of all this?" Jeff asked Lynn.

"Positive." Lynn's straight hair brushed her cheek as she nodded very slightly. Her candid gray eyes were fastened on Jeff's and she looked as serious as though she were being interrogated in court.

Jeff whistled softly. "What are you going to do?"

"I'm going to go down and tell Sergeant Cudahy."

Judy took a step forward, sensing adventure. "How about if we go along?" She shifted the oil can she was holding from her right hand to her left and wiped her greasy fingers on her dungarees. "I've never been in a police station."

Lynn looked as though she thought maybe three would be a crowd, and even Jeff, though itching to go along and be in at the kill, looked dubious. "Oh, come on!" Judy urged him. "After all, we found the puppies, didn't we? We have an interest in this case!"

"Finding is scarcely the word," said Jeff. "We waylaid them." Still considering, he turned again to Lynn. "How are you going to get to town? There isn't any morning bus."

Lynn shrugged off the two and a half miles. "Walk."

Judy played her ace. "Jeff could ride you on his handle bars," she said.

That seemed to settle it. Still in her dungarees and work shirt, Judy trundled her partially oiled bicycle out of the garage. Lynn capitulated graciously, but before they were halfway down the drive it was obvious that skirts were ill designed for handle-bar-riding; the hem of Lynn's dress kept tangling with the spokes of the front wheel. Once started, though, there was no turning Judy back. It was with Lynn riding Judy's bike and Judy perched on the handle bars of her twin's Red Indian that the trio approached the center of town.

4

As JEFF SAID LATER, they made their first mistake in bursting into the police station as they did—Judy with the legs of her soiled dungarees rolled to the knee and those absurd pigtails sticking out at right angles; Lynn with her fair hair disheveled and her face flushed. "And you," Judy added, "with a streak of dirt like a ribbon across your nose!"

Anyway, they raced up the steps and into the dim, brown, stale-smelling room from the bright summer sunshine and then stood blinking to accustom their eyes to the gloom.

"Well?"

A voice from a desk which was a vague outline near the opposite wall rapped out the word and all three of them jumped. Judy felt suddenly tongue-tied, but Lynn moved forward slowly. "Is Sergeant Cudahy in?"

"Nope." Still the twins could barely see the speaker, who appeared just a fat shape with a sharp bass voice. "Whaddayou want with Cudahy?"

Lynn hesitated to tell the entire complicated story to a stranger, particularly to such a gruff and inhospitable officer of the law as this. "I—I just wanted to see him," she stammered, "about a couple of dogs."

"Lost?"

"No, found," Judy wanted to say, but thought better of it.

"Well," Lynn started, fidgeting uncomfortably, "it's really about four dogs."

"Four! Whaddayou have, a kennel?"

Lynn took a deep breath and searched frantically for a soothing reply, when, to the intense relief of the twins as well as herself, Sergeant Cudahy stamped into the room.

Cudahy was under the same disadvantage in the sudden gloom that his visitors had encountered. He sniffed cigar smoke from the desk in the corner, but he didn't see Lynn or the Sutherlands before he groaned: "If I haven't had a rotten morning! *Everything's* gone sour."

It was certainly no time to approach the sergeant with a garbled and excited tale about dewclaws, but with the customary impatience of the young that is exactly what the three did. They pounced on him like an old friend. They rained words upon him in a torrent, the twins taking up where Lynn, whom they considered less articulate than themselves, left off. Cudahy, his mind in a whirl, felt beset. He broke through the excited children who hemmed him in and pounded his fist on the rail. In his own territory he could be peremptory. "What are you driving at?" he bawled.

Jeff sensed the situation then. "Lynn just wants another chance to examine the two puppies Mr. Gross took home with him," he said with comparative calmness. "You see, if they don't have dewclaws and hers do, it would mean—"

"Look here!" the sergeant shouted, "I haven't got any time to go gallivanting around the countryside examinin' puppies' toes. I got work to do! I'm a busy man." He looked from one to another of the youngsters who were besieging him and a deep bass chuckle from behind the cigar smoke in the corner only irritated him the more. Without that chuckle, Judy thought, he might even then have relented, but now he felt called upon to prove his mettle. He turned to Lynn. "You got two dogs, ain't you?"

"Yes, but—"

"O.K. Gross has got two dogs too. So that's that. Now you kids git! And don't come back. I never heard such a pack of foolishness in my life!"

Cudahy meant it. There was no appeal from the tone of that voice. The twins, followed by Lynn, turned finally and left the room. Jeff tripped over a cuspidor in the hall, which made him feel even more gauche and adolescent than he had in the interview with the policeman, but Judy sailed down the steps to the main street with her chin in the air. "Well, of all the insulting treatment!" she said quite audibly.

Jeff, feeling like a properly spanked child, looked

at his indignant twin in astonishment, and then his whole face broke into a grin. Standing there in her old loafers and rolled-up jeans, the shoulders of the man's work shirt slipping off her back, eyes flashing and pigtails bristling, Judy looked like a furious child. And her voice, imitating the offended dignity of an older woman, was at strange odds with her appearance. "What are you going to do about it?" Jeff asked.

Lynn looked as deflated as a pricked balloon, but even her brother's effort to make her face reality failed

to mollify Judy. She kicked up the standard of her bike and faced it toward the center of town, forgetting that Lynn had been riding it on the way into Wayne. Her expression changed from indignation to dedication. "From now on," she said dramatically, "we can expect no help from the police!"

If she could have then mounted the bicycle—though she would have preferred a white horse—and ridden rapidly away, Judy might have felt that she had achieved an effect. But of course with Jeff there such a thing was impossible. Sometimes she found it very embarrassing to have a twin.

Judy's feet were no more than on the pedals when he said: "Uh-uh. Not so fast. It's Lynn that goes forward alone, remember. You ride with me, peanut." And there Judy was, ignominiously forced to arrange herself on Jeff's handle bars, after which all three of them rode rather quietly back home.

Looking at it from a man's standpoint, Jeff could see Cudahy's point of view. He felt embarrassed and a little ashamed that he should have been persuaded so easily into this morning's expedition. He'd told Judy last night he was finished with the whole affair. Why hadn't he stuck to his guns instead of getting involved with a couple of hysterical females? For Lynn, in her quiet, half-apologetic way, was obviously even more upset than Judy. Jeff could see her white, set face out of the corner of his eye. There was something about the girl that aroused his sympathy, yet at the same time he felt baffled and irritated.

"Oh, forget it, Lynn!" he said finally. "After all, what difference does it make?"

And Lynn made the same answer she had on the previous afternoon. "Oh, but you don't understand!" she cried. "It makes all the difference in the world!"

5 M UCH AGAINST HIS WILL, Jeff found himself, on the very afternoon of the police-station episode, riding along the road which led to Gross Point.

Judy was his companion on this expedition, and it was at her instigation that it had been started at all. Jeff still didn't know quite how he'd got involved, but he did know that when

Judy's sympathies were aroused she could be very beguiling, even if she was his twin. At any rate, for the second time Jeff had broken a promise he'd made to himself—to stay out of this silly affair of the black cocker spaniels. Here he was, disgruntled yet acquiescent, plugging up the long hill that approached the Gross estate.

At his side, near the middle of the road, Judy was standing on her pedals, anxious not to be the first to give in and push the bike uphill. She had changed from the disreputable dungarees to a clean seersucker play suit, and the red bows which tied her re-braided pigtails matched the stripe of the cotton. Never again, she'd decided, would she be betrayed by

her appearance, as she considered she had been in the morning. From now on she intended to dress like a lady—in public, at least.

"D'you think," she asked Jeff between laboring breaths, "that I look older if I let my hair hang?"

Her twin, who was busy berating himself that he was on the road to Gross Point at all, said: "Huh? Hang? What?"

"Oh, never mind!" Boys—all boys, even Jeff— could sometimes be so dumb.

Jeff, unconscious that he had failed his sister, slid from the seat of the bike and started to push, so Judy felt she could give up too. She moved out of the center of the road in case a car should round the bend above and fell companionably into step with the boy, though their thoughts were far apart.

"Why," Jeff asked after a while, "do you suppose Lynn is so secretive?"

"I think that's 'se*cr*etive,' " said Judy thoughtfully. She and her mother made it their business to jack Jeff up on his pronunciation and it always seemed out of character to her twin that with Judy's impulsive, slap-dash nature she should be such a stickler for pronunci-ation. "I don't know," she went on, once this was off her mind. "I believe in Lynn, but I can't figure her out."

"You don't even try," accused Jeff. "You're warm-hearted and friendly and you take people on faith. Dad says that's going to get you into trouble someday.

Why would it make all the difference in the world if the sets of pups should be mixed up? Why can't Lynn explain? She keeps saying, 'You don't understand.' Of course we don't. How can we?"

Judy shook her head. "We can't. But you could see as well as I could how worried Lynn looked. I do feel sorry for her. I can't help it."

"What's Mr. Gross going to think when we traipse in there?" Jeff asked glumly.

"Think? He won't think anything at all. What could be more natural than that we'd want to stop and see the puppies we rescued?" Judy waved her arm with an inclusive gesture. "Anyway, it's the middle of the afternoon. He probably won't be home. We probably won't even see him." She considered a minute. "I think it would be better, though," she added, "if we didn't say anything about the fifth toes."

Jeff, who rarely shared Judy's vivid desire for adventure, grunted. He didn't quite see how they were going to investigate the matter of the missing dewclaws without making it pretty obvious to any bystander just what was going on. He walked on a few steps, then said as much.

"Poof!" Judy blew his objection away lightly. "I can pick up one of the pups, or even play with him on the ground, and run my hand along his front legs."

"Under all those feathers, do you think you could tell?" Jeff sounded dubious.

"I think so. Anyway, we'll just have to take a chance."

They were on level ground again now, directly in front of the open iron gates which led into Gross Point. The name of the house was carved into the gray-stone pillars which supported the huge gates and a curving white-stone drive led up an avenue of trees. The twins mounted their bikes again and rode in. Neither had ever been inside the gate before, and the house, as they approached it, looked very sumptuous and impressive in comparison to their own simple colonial-type home. It wasn't extremely large, but it was built in French-château style, and a side terrace dropped to a swimming pool which was lined with sky-blue tiles. The three-car garage, separate from the house, was on the far side, and behind this building Judy and Jeff could glimpse the runs of a good-sized kennel.

"Looks like something out of Hollywood," Jeff muttered, and Judy nodded, saying, "There doesn't seem to be anyone home."

The house indeed lay very quiet in the afternoon sunshine. Only the crunch of bicycle wheels on the pebbled drive disturbed the calm. Where a walk separated near the pool to surround the house the twins turned their wheels with one accord to the rear, making straight for the kennels. A gardener, clipping hedge, nodded to them, but there seemed to be no kennelman about. "Let's just park and see if we can find our pups before anybody shows up," Judy suggested. "It'd be easier that way."

Trying to appear quite casual but feeling a little uncomfortable now that they were on the spot, the twins leaned their bikes against the trunk of a huge oak tree which spread over the drive, and sauntered down the path which led to the kennels. It wasn't a long path, but Judy felt that it stretched endlessly before her. She wanted to run, to seek out the two special pups, to get at them before anyone caught her. All the confidence she had felt that Mr. Gross would welcome their visit vanished into thin air. To measure her steps, to keep a grip on her impulse to hurry, was almost impossibly hard.

Jeff, oddly, felt less like a trespasser than Judy. Now that he was here it seemed perfectly natural that he should be walking down this path to the kennels. He squinted his eyes against the sun and from the medley of dogs which jumped, barking, against the wire tried to pick out the two black pups. Suddenly he saw them.

"There they are!"

"Where?"

"In the end run—nearest us. They're alone." He'd expected them to be back with their litter brothers and sisters. He hadn't been looking for them in a run by themselves.

"Are you sure?" Black spaniel puppies, to Judy, could look so much alike—

"Almost." Softly Jeff whistled. "Here, Shadow! Here, Sambo!"

The pups came at once, wagging their tails and putting their forepaws high against the fence which penned them in. From the next run three other puppies, two black and one red, joined in their delighted barks of greeting. The twins glanced at these others briefly. They seemed about the same age—probably these were the litter mates—but they weren't half so handsome, even to untrained eyes, as the sturdy black boys in the end run.

"I guess you're right," Judy admitted. Then she added in a louder tone for the benefit of a possible unseen audience: "Aren't they sweet? Do you think they remember us, Jeff? I wonder if Mr. Gross would mind if we let them out just for a minute?" Her hand, already on the latch to the kennel door, belied her words. Anticipation was so great that her fingers fumbled—

"Stop that!" The words could have been shot from a gun, so loud was their report on the twins. Judy jumped and her hand flew off the latch spontaneously as Jeff whirled around to face Mr. Gross.

The stout man looked apoplectic with anger and a vein twitched rhythmically in his red forehead. "Just what do you think you're up to?" he yelled.

Jeff recovered himself at once. "We stopped by to see the puppies, sir," he said mildly. "We didn't see you around, so—"

Judy's breath was still coming in short pumps, but she had to admire Jeff's poise. In a pinch she could always count on her brother. He made their visit seem utterly reasonable and friendly, in a few commonplace words.

But if Jeff's explanation seemed reasonable to Judy it had the opposite effect on their host. "So you thought you'd sneak down here!" Mr. Gross shouted. "So you thought you'd let out the dogs!" He glared at Jeff, his shaggy eyebrows bristling as though they were attached to individual wires and his thick neck bulging out over his shirt collar.

"We didn't 'sneak,'" Judy piped up, feeling more righteous than she had any call to.

"There's a sign by the road that says, 'No Trespassing'!" Mr. Gross went on, ignoring the girl. "Can't you read?"

"We were just—" Jeff started, but the big man's voice drowned his words. "This is private property, understand? *Private property*. And I don't intend to have any nosy kids fooling around my kennels. You can get off this place and stay off, and if I catch you sneaking around here again I'll call the police."

Never in her life had Judy been addressed in such a manner. Her throat burned with impotent rage, and she felt that if she tried to defend herself she'd burst into angry tears. Jeff, on the other hand, seemed to be growing cooler by the instant. He made no further attempt at an explanation until Gross had entirely finished his ranting monologue. Then he said: "We'll go. Don't worry! But before we go I just want you to get this straight. We weren't planning to steal your pups. We just wanted to play with them. Heck! If we returned them yesterday I can't understand why you'd think we'd want to steal them today."

Judy's eyes were on Gross's face, and for some reason Jeff's words seemed to surprise him. He grew perceptibly calmer, and when Jeff turned to his sister and said, "Come on, Judy," he blocked the path back to the bikes.

"Wait a minute!" Gross's shoe-button eyes narrowed, and he looked directly at Judy, whose hand he had seen on the latch to the pen door. "You wanted to get at those dogs bad," he said in a voice that was now more insinuating than threatening. "Why?"

Judy's eyes dropped. Instinctively honest, she couldn't say, "Just to play with them," with the proper conviction. Mr. Gross, she knew, would recognize at once that she was lying. Yet to do the obvious thing and explain Lynn's theory about the dewclaws seemed useless. He'd never let them examine the pups now! Besides, that would be admitting an ulterior motive for paying this call and would give the kennel owner some grounds for his accusations. She stammered, "I —I was only . . ." Then she looked helplessly at Jeff.

"We've told you that we wanted to play with the pups." Jeff's conscience appeared untroubled by this half-truth. As he faced Mr. Gross his aversion for the man was increasing. Something entirely apart from the insults he had hurled at them made Jeff distrust the master of Gross Point. Only once before had he felt this same way, when, as a grammar-school child he'd seen an angry huckster beat his horse. He'd hated that huckster with a fury that had frightened him. He'd wanted to kick him and claw him, to hurt him as he had hurt the bewildered horse. In the same way he was frightened now of his own emotion. He wanted to get Judy out of here—away from this repulsive fat man—back to their own safe, pleasant house. He moved toward his sister and took her arm. "Come on. He told us to get out. Let's get. What are we waiting for?"

Mr. Gross showed no intention of getting off the path, but the twins skirted his hulk by way of the grass. They walked quickly to their wheels and mounted while the kennel owner, backed by yapping dogs, watched them from a distance. Jeff looked back just once, and he could have sworn that there was now more curiosity than anger in the fat man's eyes.

ON THE PENNSYL-vania Dutch water bench which stood in the entrance hall of the Sutherlands' house lay a penciled note for Judy, in the handwriting of Willie-Belle, the laundress. Beside it lay a man's battered felt hat.

Judy noticed both of them at once. She didn't recognize the hat, but she could hear voices, one her father's and one a stranger's, coming from the small study at the right of the hall. She went over and read the note at once.

"A Mrs. Tomass," she read in Willie-Belle's painful scrawl, "wants you should come and stay with her baby tomorrow night."

That would be Mrs. Thomas, Judy knew, and she tucked the note into the pocket of her play suit with the mental promise to call her as soon as she found out what was going on in the study. Living as far out in the country as the Sutherlands did, it was rather unusual that Judy's father should be closeted with a visitor just at dinnertime. A mild clatter of utensils in the kitchen and a whiff of freshly baked apple pie led Judy to her mother. "Who's in the study with Dad?" she asked at once.

"Oh, hello, dear! Is Jeff with you? Will you please put some butter on the butter plates and pour the water? Dinner's almost ready." Mrs. Sutherland stooped to peek into the oven of the electric stove, then nodded in satisfaction and shut it hastily.

Judy picked up a paring knife and went to the refrigerator for the butter before she repeated, "Who's with Dad, Mommy?"

"With your father? Oh, Mr. Matthews. They've been in there for the last half hour. I don't know what it's all about."

"Mr. Matthews?" Judy's eyes widened. "Lynn's father?"

"Yes, dear, of course. Please hurry with the butter, Judy. This soufflé's almost done. And you might open some of that grape jam. It's good with cheese."

Judy went about these mundane tasks dreamily, reflecting on this new turn of events. If the grownups were getting involved in this affair of the spaniels— for she had leaped to the immediate conclusion that this was the cause of Mr. Matthews' visit—something exciting really was afoot.

The kitchen door banged behind Jeff while Judy was pouring water into the goblets. She could scarcely wait to tell him who was here. As soon as he had greeted his mother and walked on through to the dining room she said: "Hsst! Lynn's father is in the study with Dad!"

Jeff greeted this information by raising his eyebrows and looking interested. As the twins had coasted down the hill from Gross Point they'd come to an important conclusion—that they were going to see this spaniel mystery through.

For even Jeff now admitted that it *was* a mystery. It simply wasn't reasonable that a man of wealth and position should fly into a rage because a couple of kids paid a visit to a pair of pups they had rescued. It didn't make sense that he'd been so suspicious of Judy's attempt to open the kennel gate. All along Lynn's insistence that the dogs found marching down the road belonged to her had bothered Jeff. It all added up to something peculiar—something very peculiar indeed. Slow though he was to be aroused, cautious in taking sides, once Jeff's mind was made up he was a loyal ally, and he was ready from now on to stand by Lynn. He wished he knew more about Mr. Gross—and more, for that matter about Lynn and her father. He must remember to ask his dad—

But just now his mother was calling, "Dinner!" and the front door had already shut behind his father's guest. Judy was carrying the cheese soufflé, puffy and golden, in to the table, and it was time for the family to assemble. Jeff pulled out the Hepplewhite armchair in which his mother always sat and held it for her.

Judy slipped into her seat and looked impatiently toward her dad. Mr. Sutherland settled his napkin on his lap, said a simple grace, then glanced down the length of the table at his flushed and attractive wife.

"Sheila," he said slowly, confirming Jeff's reasoning and Judy's hunch, "there seems to be more to this affair of the lost puppies than meets the eye."

Judy opened her mouth, but shut it again when she caught Jeff's glance. She knew as well as her brother that her dad could never be rushed, but it was all she could do to control the flood of questions that threatened to overflow her quick mind.

"Really, George?" Mrs. Sutherland served the vegetables as she replied. "Whatever makes you think that, dear? Something Mike Matthews said?" Then she turned to her daughter and went right on in the same tone of voice: "I left the hot biscuits in the oven, Judy. Will you get them?"

Judy dawdled on her way to the kitchen, anxious not to miss a word of her father's reply. But she needn't have been so cautious. Mr. Sutherland intended to see his family properly launched on their dinner before he settled down to what was rather a long story.

"Jam, Jeff?"

"No, thanks, Dad."

"These are the first of our own tomatoes, George."

Judy thought the trivial family mealtime chatter would never end. Closing her eyes to Jeff's negative

signals, she risked a mild reminder. "What about Mr. Matthews, Dad?"

"Oh, before you get started on that," interrupted Mrs. Sutherland, while the twins seethed, "I must tell you—Mamam phoned this afternoon. She's coming tomorrow to stay with us for a while."

"Mamam?" Judy's interest was temporarily deflected and her voice rose on the name. It brought to her mind a picture of a straight-backed little old lady with an erect head topped by a knot of sparse gray hair, blue eyes as alert as a sparrow's, and a memory that went back and back and back to the dim days just following the Civil War. She didn't know quite what relation Mamam was to Jeff and herself, but she always thought of her as her grandmother, because she knew that when her real grandmother had died, Mamam had raised her mother. "Oh, good!" Judy said approvingly. Then her glance returned to her dad. "But about Mr. Matthews . . ."

George Sutherland's eyes twinkled and he leaned back in his chair. "Tenacity," he said, thoughtfully, "is a quality shared by most women." He seemed about to launch on a philosophical discourse.

Judy squirmed forward. "O Daddy, stop teasing!"

Mr. Sutherland capitulated suddenly. "All right, Judy, but I may as well tell you in advance that Mike Matthews' story doesn't prove anything, as far as the cocker mix-up is concerned. He apparently just came to me for advice—perhaps because I'm a lawyer . . ." His voice trailed off as he bit into a biscuit. "I'm afraid I wasn't much help," he added after a while.

"Mr. Matthews used to be Mr. Gross's gardener, didn't he?" Judy prompted impatiently.

"He was also his kennelman," her father nodded, and the twins' eyes widened in surprise. "About a year after Matthews started working at Gross Point, Mr. Gross got interested in breeding cockers as a hobby. Matthews knew something about dogs, and Gross drafted him as helper when his first kennels were built. Since then, Mike says, they've been expanded into something rather fabulous."

Judy wanted to say, "They're awfully big and expensive-looking." She could see again the neat concrete runs which backed on the three-winged frame bungalow which housed the dogs. In the moment before Mr. Gross had accosted them that afternoon she'd glimpsed, through the windows, a trophy room at one end and a kitchen at the other. But Jeff was shaking his head to keep her from interrupting.

"According to Matthews, however," Mr. Sutherland continued leisurely, "Mr. Gross never had great success with his cockers outside of local shows. I don't pretend to know anything about dog-breeding, but

Matthews says it's a long, slow process to build up a noteworthy kennel, even if you have all the money in the world to spend. It seems Gross has big ambitions. He wants to own a cocker that can win at Madison Square Garden—a dog that will become as famous as My Own Brucie was back in the thirties. Well, of course, that's flying pretty high!"

"Madison Square Garden? My Own Brucie?" Judy's forehead wrinkled in a puzzled frown.

"Madison Square is where the big New York Dog Show's held," Jeff helped his sister out.

"Brucie was the black cocker who used to win, one year after another," murmured Mrs. Sutherland, and Judy thanked her with an admiring glance. What a lot older people sometimes knew!

"Anyway," Mr. Sutherland went on, "Matthews recommended to Mr. Gross a breeding plan that would cover years and that might eventually give him a really outstanding dog. Gross turned the idea down flat. He's always been impatient in business and he's used to getting what he wants—fast! He told Matthews to go out and *buy* a dog. Matthews apparently claimed it couldn't be done, and the two men quarreled."

"Was that when Mr. Matthews got fired?" Judy asked.

"No. I imagine Mr. Gross is canny. He knew he had a good thing in Matthews. Maybe he thought he could still win him over. But then, one day, according to Mike, Mr. Gross kicked a dog in a fit of temper. Mike admits he lost his head and slugged Gross, and, of course, that was the end.

"Maybe I shouldn't say it was the end, because Matthews claims that Gross, with an ugly sense of revenge, did his best to ruin his chances to get another job. Mr. Gross is a powerful man. It wouldn't be a hard thing to do. At any rate, Matthews landed next at that old, run-down Carstairs' place. Then, when Miss Carstairs moved away, he began to take day's work, and that's what he's doing now."

Mr. Sutherland put down his fork and sighed. "Of course that's only one side of the picture," he said with his accustomed fair-mindedness. "Artemus Gross might have quite a different tale to spin."

Judy looked shocked. "O Daddy! You don't think Mr. Matthews was—was lying?"

Her father smiled gently. "I wouldn't like to think so, dear. But I don't *know*." He understood Judy's youthful desire to champion the underdog, but his cautious lawyer's mind told him that none of them, really, had any right to judge.

"But what did Mr. Matthews have to say about the pups we found?" Jeff wanted to get the end of the story.

"Just this. He's sure the dogs you found on the road are his, and that the ones now in his pen don't belong to him at all. He can't produce papers. He won't even tell me how he came to get them. But he seems to think his cockers were going to develop into pretty fine dogs, and that they're now sitting up in the kennel at Gross Point."

"Well," Mrs. Sutherland ejaculated, "if that isn't the most fantastic story!"

The twins, entirely aware of this conclusion, looked unsurprised. "What did Mr. Matthews want you to do, Dad?" Jeff asked.

"I don't think he quite knew himself. Maybe he felt that because you and Judy were involved it would be a good idea to get his side of the story straight in my mind. Maybe he hoped I'd offer to go see Gross. I don't know."

"Did he tell you about the dewclaws?" Judy asked.

"Dewclaws? No. He told me that if he could get a chance to examine the two pups that are up at Gross Point he was pretty sure he could identify them, but he didn't mention dewclaws."

It was Judy's turn to tell the story of their afternoon excursion. She dramatized it, tumbling one word on top of another in a breathless gush. Jeff was aware, before she was half through, that his father was frowning heavily, but Judy was completely unconscious of her parent's reaction. She hurried right on to the end.

"I'm glad you told me all this, Judith," said her father in a deceptively calm voice. "It may have taught you and Jeff that it's far wiser to stay out of other people's business than to meddle."

"But, Daddy," Judy cried, "you do believe Mr. Matthews, don't you? After this afternoon—"

"I just don't know." Her father spoke the words with consideration. His daughter's story of the expedition to Gross Point seemed to prejudice Mr. Sutherland against the gardener, rather than for him. "At best Matthews has a rather thin tale to spin. For all I know this feud between him and his former employer may have led Matthews to steal the original cockers from Gross. It's a pretty hopeless tangle, and one that I'd like to stay out of. Now let's drop the subject. That's that!"

Judy, without her father's order to drop the subject, would have denied hotly the premise that it might be Mr. Matthews, and not Mr. Gross, who was a thief. But she recognized a finality in her dad's voice from which there was no appeal. Silently she helped her mother to clear the table for dessert.

Jeff, toying with the silver spoon in the salt boat, was weighing his father's disinclination to judge with Judy's warm loyalty to Lynn Matthews. For once, though he admired his dad's fine judicial mind, his adult and masculine attitude of keeping clear of such a hopeless mix-up, Jeff's sympathies tallied with his sister's. The imprint of the unpleasant interview at Gross Point was still fresh. He, Jeff, would like to show that big, fat bozo a thing or two!

In the kitchen Judy, rinsing the dinner plates, felt a paper crackle in the pocket of her play suit. It was

Willie-Belle's misspelled note, and it drew her thoughts from the black spaniel mystery to the everyday business of living. She must remember to call Mrs. Thomas right after dinner!

Mrs. Thomas, she found when she went to the phone, was wondering if Judy could come and stay with small Toby tomorrow night while she and her husband went to the movies. They'd go to the first show, she promised hastily, so that Judy wouldn't be out too late. Baby sitters, as Toby's mother well knew, were gold nuggets in this neck of the woods, and worthy of considerate handling.

"Certainly I'll come!" To Judy, still quite new at this method of picking up pin money, a job was a job, and to be greeted not with reluctance but with cheers. "If you'll let me know what time you'll be home, I'll ask Jeff to walk up the hill for me." The Thomases lived in a small white tenant house on the estate nearly opposite Gross Point. The place was like a doll's house, with a living room full of shabby chintz and bright new books, and Judy always liked to go there.

"Shall we say ten-thirty?" came Mrs. Thomas' pleasant voice.

"Ten-thirty will be fine."

Hanging the receiver on its hook, Judy went to find Jeff.

"Sure, I'll come get you," Jeff promised readily. He was sitting on the terrace untangling a fishing line, and he looked up at her slyly. "I ought to charge a fee for services, though. Say ten per cent?"

"I'd rather walk home alone," Judy flung back.

"Mother would never let you."

"You don't know."

"I'll bet!"

It was the sort of teasing, brother-sister bickering that Judy had grown up with. Sometimes she wondered what it would be like to be an only child, to have no one with whom to scrap and share things. In her relationship with Jeff there was more sharing than scrapping. She still considered him more fun than any other boy she knew.

She walked back into the house, disdaining to carry the argument farther, but she grinned at him over her shoulder and he wrinkled his nose and grinned back at her. People missed something, Judy thought, who weren't twins.

The next day, however, she fell to wishing that she were the other half of this particular twin combination. The temperature hovered at ninety, the air was damp and sticky, and Jeff jaunted off with his fishing rod to pick up Bill Rogers, the lad next door, and hike over to Hopkins' Pond. Judy, meanwhile, was left home to help her mother to clean the guest room for Mamam.

Expending the least possible effort, she pushed the mop over the random-width floor boards slowly. Even her affection for the old lady who was to use the room failed to stimulate any enthusiasm for her job. She dusted with equal lassitude, pausing by the casement windows which looked out on the Rogers' place, beyond which were green fields hazy with heat. From far away, in the direction of the Matthews', she could hear the muted barking of a dog. It was just a ghost of a sound when it reached her, scarcely louder than a heartbeat, but it set her to wondering again about Lynn and the two unwanted puppies in the Matthews' pen. It was dreadful that they should be unwanted, through no fault of their own. She hoped Lynn was kind to them. But of course she was!

"Judy! Will you bring me the furniture polish when you finish with it?"

"Yes, Mother." Judy sighed. In books the heroines always had time for reflection—time to brood or dream or spend all their time tracking down clues. That was the trouble with this homemade mystery of the cocker spaniels. It wasn't a real mystery at all, because there weren't any clues.

Except for the dewclaws—

Something made Judy cling to an avid desire to find out about those dewclaws. If they really were missing on the pups at Gross Point—

"Yes, Mother, I'm hurrying!" she called, but, sinking down on the slipper chair at the foot of the bed, she put her head in both hands.

7

Moonlight flood-
ed the Thomas cottage
with steel-blue drifts of
color. In the garden
crickets chirped, prophesying heat. A stray cat slipped
across the roadway, bent on adventure. An owl hooted
eerily, but though the sound carried quite plainly
through the open windows, Judy did not hear it. She
was sitting with her feet curled under her in the corner of a chintz-covered love seat completely absorbed
in a book.

Toby Thomas, thirteen months old, had long since
stopped shouting his strident "A-da's" from the nurs-
ery upstairs and had dropped off to sleep in a crib
from which he had flung both pad and sheet. Downstairs the mantel clock ticked calmly away, and Judy
turned the pages of the book busily. She was never in
the least afraid in an empty house in the country: only
the city with its noise and bustle made her heart pump
with fear. From time to time she glanced at the clock,
wishing she could make it tick more slowly. Now that
she'd found this book, she wanted to get through it
before the Thomases came home.

It was a red book, quite fat. Judy had found it among some books on dog-training on the bottom shelf of one of the bookcases which flanked the fireplace. In a faded gold border on the cover was printed the title: *The Cocker Spaniel.*

First of all Judy had leafed through it busily, trying to find something about dewclaws, but no reference was made to them in the chapter on the raising of puppies, nor could she discover their mention elsewhere in the book. This was disappointing, of course, but the book was so crowded with photographs of cockers that Judy soon forgot her regret in studying them. Red cockers, black-and-white ones, pure blacks! So many dogs, with such fancy names. "CH. Bellmore Buffkins, CH. Rowcliffe Miracle, CH. My Own Red Brucie." Judy studied the last picture intently. Maybe this was some relative of the black Brucie her father had been talking about. Almost every dog, she noted, had those mysterious letters, CH., in front of their elaborate names. Jeff, or maybe her dad, would know what they meant. She must remember to ask.

There was one picture, of a dog named "My Own Right of Way," which reminded her of Shadow and Sambo. He looked older, and his coat was very full and heavy, but he had the same spirited lift to his head, the same sparkle in the one eye which showed in the photograph. It would be fun to have a dog like that!

The clock struck ten, and a car pulled into the shallow drive. The movie must have been a short one, for the Thomases were home early. Regretfully Judy put the red book back on the shelf. She could hear the friends who had picked them up call, "Good night," and the sound of the engine as the car backed and pulled away.

"Hello, Judy. Everything been all right?"

"Yes, indeed!" Judy turned from the bookcase and smiled at plump, dumpy Mrs. Thomas, who had soft blue eyes and fading orange hair. "Toby's always good. Isn't he getting to be a big boy!"

Any praise of her son always delighted the little woman. She beamed at Judy, opening her pocketbook to pay her the usual fee. "Mr. Thomas will walk down the hill with you, dear."

"Oh, no!" Judy protested, almost too heartily. She shot a glance in the direction of the man of the house, who was dark and bespectacled, and with whom Judy always felt rather ill at ease because she considered him studious and peculiar. "That won't be necessary," she went on more mildly. "Jeff's meeting me. He'll be on his way up now." The clock told her that Jeff wouldn't be likely to appear for a good half hour, but that didn't worry her in the least. A time alone in the moonlight was an intriguing idea. She wasn't in the least afraid.

"Wouldn't you rather wait here? Your mother—"

"Oh, Mother won't mind!" Judy said confidently.

"I'll just walk along and meet him. It's a beautiful night!"

Finally the amenities were over, and she was out on the road, with the moonlight swimming across the valley where home lay and not a sound, other than the background music of the crickets, to disturb the peace.

Judy breathed deeply. A sense of enchantment was in the moon-washed air. Great oaks and poplars threw their shadows across the road, and the evening dew made the fields smell fresh and somehow exciting. Imagine, Judy thought, being scared to be out alone on a night like this!

The heels of her loafers made small clicking sounds on the macadam road as Judy walked along. The lamps of the Thomas house were hidden quickly behind the high hedge which screened the cottage from the road, and on the opposite side of the highway two stone pillars gleamed in the blue light. The shadows of a great iron gate, opened wide, fell in long bars across a white-stone drive. Suddenly Judy stopped and looked up. She could barely read the chiseled letters, but she knew them well. Gross Point!

For Judy the enchantment of the still night died, and in its place rose a spontaneous idea which both terrified and intrigued her. Suppose—suppose she could find out about the dewclaws alone—now! Suppose, guided by the moonlight, yet keeping in the shadow of the trees, she could creep along the grass beside the drive, round the house to the kennel, call the puppies softly. They knew her. They would come to her. Her small hands clenched and her fingers felt clammy. There must be twenty minutes left of the half hour. Before Jeff came whistling up the hill there would be time. . . .

Fascinated, she stared at the bars of the gate lying black across the drive. The moonlight no longer seemed friendly. The bars made it sinister and frightening to be out alone. A chill ran down Judy's spine, and she shook herself and tried to walk on. The idea that had flooded into her brain was ridiculous, one that Jeff wouldn't entertain for a moment. If she had been accused of trespassing in broad daylight, what could she be accused of at night? Yet she was still standing rooted to the spot, and beyond the bars stretched the white sweep of the drive, inviting, beckoning. It would take such a few moments of courage, and in return she would *know*. . . . Quick as a cat, Judy slipped through the gate into the shelter of the curving line of trees.

Once inside, it was simply a matter of going forward soundlessly from tree to tree. Judy stayed on the turf, knowing that her shoes on the crushed stone of the driveway would make a crunch that might give her away. Sound effects, at this moment, were something to be avoided. Against each trunk she paused for a moment, a thin black shadow, hugging the tree, listening. Her awareness seemed especially acute, and she had presence of mind enough to be glad that the neutral blue of her chambray dress faded into gray in the dark.

As she drew closer to the house she could pick out the round black shadows of the boxwood which lined the encircling walk. Rhododendrons flanked the broad steps to the terrace, but they remained in shadow, because at the front of the mansion there was no light. Judy's heart was throbbing now. Her mouth was as dry as parchment, and she was feeling strangely sick at her stomach without recognizing it as a symptom of fear. Each advance to the next tree trunk increased her trepidation. Bells hummed in her ears and beads of perspiration, not induced by the warmth of the night, sprang to her forehead. All that could happen swam in front of her eyes. She'd been a fool—a complete and utter fool, a baby, an idiot, to have been led by an impulse to attempt such a thing!

Yet now that she had started, it never occurred to Judy to turn back. Not even when she reached the last of the trees that bordered the inside curve of the drive and realized that somehow she must cross the broad, moonlit expanse of crushed stone that led to the box-lined flagstone walk did she really falter. With a quick gesture she reached down and pulled off her loafers, tucking them under her left arm. Crouched close to the tree she studied the course she must take.

The kennels, she remembered clearly, lay at the back of the house to the right. The drive she had been following approached from the left, swept to a turnaround at the garage, which was situated next to the kennel, and then on down to some rear entrance gate at which Judy could only guess. On this near side of the house were the flower gardens and pool, with few trees to cast shadows. On the garage side, she was almost sure, the low, spreading dogwoods and Japanese cherries gave way to maples and pine.

If she crossed the drive here, it was easy to see, she would be in full moonlight. If she went on, chancing the stretch of lawn in front of the terrace steps, the trees near the garage would offer shelter and shadow. Still, she was familiar with this side of the house, with the path that led to the kennels, while of the other side she knew nothing. It was a hard decision to make.

Reflection decided her to risk the unknown rather than the moonlight. She clung with one arm to the trunk of the tree where she had stopped while she tried to steady her breathing. She'd need all the breath she could hoard for this sprint across the moonlit lawn. As she waited she was reminded of a time she and Jeff and a crowd of their friends had played "hide-and-seek" in the garden at night. She remembered the shudders that had overcome her as she crouched under black bushes, the fingers that might reach out and touch her. It hadn't been much better, even, when she was "it." Then there was the horrid feeling that all around were the hidden, ready to dash out of the blackness, ready to yell as they raced for base. Judy shivered, and with her left arm gripped her loafers tighter. This is ridiculous, she tried to tell herself. I'll count to ten and then I'll go.

"One — two — three — four — five — six — seven — eight — nine —"

She reached the far tree, panting, crouching low to the ground. Her breathing sounded loud and labored in her ears. She'd been right! This far side of the house was indeed in deep shadow. Yet from long French windows, curved at the top, there came a sweep of light!

The light lay in broad strips on the stone terrace, which extended around this side of the house. A good bit of the terrace was in the shadow of the wide leafy branches of a big oak which dominated the turnaround. Behind this enormous black umbrella the

moon was completely hidden. This had indeed been the wiser course.

Very gently Judy eased forward. She had no curiosity about the light. She only wished to avoid it. Soft-footed, she sprinted across the drive, scarcely noticing that the pebbles cut sharply through her ankle socks. She dropped in the shelter of a hedge which flanked this side terrace and, bent almost double, hurried along it. The kennels would be just beyond. . . .

At that instant a door slammed sharply at the back of the house and a dead twig snapped under Judy's stockinged foot. All the dogs in Christendom started to bark at once!

Judy's action was quicker than thought. She lay flat and rolled quickly under the hedge, disregarding the fact that her dress was by no means an old one—oblivious, almost, to the pointed darts of barberry which pricked her arms and legs like a hundred needles. Her heart, next to the damp earth, was now pounding uncontrollably. She felt that she must be vibrating with the shock of it. Bearing the hurt of the barberry, she lay perfectly motionless, waiting for what was to come. In the distance she could hear footsteps going down a path.

Judy was lucky. The walker was going away from her, toward the kennels, perhaps, because the barking was increasing in both volume and excitement. For one clear-sighted moment she realized what uproar would have been raised had she, a stranger, approached that kennel in the dark. With all her heart she wished that she had never embarked on this mad, ill-considered adventure, that she was back on the safe macadam highway which sloped toward home.

Toward home and Jeff! What Judy wouldn't have given to see Jeff sauntering up the hill to meet her in the moonlight, hands in his pockets, whistling, the way he always did! She closed her eyes and swallowed hard.

But the whistle that just then cut through the shrill barking of the dogs wasn't Jeff's. It was sharp, peremptory. It made Judy stop trembling for a moment and lie tense, too frightened to ease out from under the prickly hedge and crawl away.

From somewhere behind the house a gate clanked shut. Then Judy heard the footsteps again, but this time they were returning, not growing fainter. The walker must be coming back.

Wedged painfully under the hedge, Judy tried to stop breathing. She drew her toes and her fingers close together and burrowed her head into the earth, trying to make herself small. Alice in Wonderland's success with the magic potion labeled "Drink Me" flashed briefly through her head. O for some such potion now!

The dogs were quieting and the walker, whoever it was, seemed to be coming in a direct line toward the spot where Judy lay. Lying on her face as she was she couldn't see a thing, but the ring of heavy heels on flagstones kept growing louder. Definitely, this was a man. A big, heavy man. Mr. Gross? Surely he couldn't have seen her, in this deep shadow! Yet he was coming on, on, on until he was so close that she could hear a squeak in one of his shoes.

And the worst thing was, he was coming up behind her. At that moment Judy became certain that there is nothing more dreadful in the world than having your back to something of which you are frightened. With her elbows pressed into her sides and her nose against the damp ground she lay paralyzed. Left, right, left, right, each second step accompanied by the creak of the shoe. Then suddenly the man stood still.

It was agony not to turn over and look up. Why was he stopping? If he'd seen her why didn't he shout? All that Judy could hear was a heavy grunt as though he were lifting a package or hitching something up under his arm. Then, just as she thought she couldn't bear it another instant, his steps started again.

In a flash she realized what he was doing. He was mounting the terrace steps just behind her—the side steps which led to the long French windows which opened like doors to this porch.

And he was carrying something weighty. Of that she was sure! For with each couple of steps he grunted again, not painfully, just as a fat man hoisting a suitcase will grunt.

When the steps struck the stone floor of the terrace above Judy dared to breathe again. Cautiously she raised her head from the earth and opened her eyes. Because her feet were toward the steps she could see nothing, but she could hear Mr. Gross's voice boom, distinctly: "Here they are, Fitz. Now look 'em over." Then a screen door slammed gently.

Judy lay exactly as she was for several seconds after Mr. Gross had entered the house. Then, gradually, she relaxed. The nearness of her escape left her incapable of thought for a time, but as her terror waned her normal curiosity began to return. Gently she detached the many-toothed sticks of barberry from her arms, but she couldn't reach her legs, so she had to roll over and let it rip, clenching her teeth to bear its torturous scratching.

"Here they are, Fitz. Now look 'em over." What could Mr. Gross have been talking about?

Right above her, Judy knew, were the long French windows, open wide to the summer night. If she could edge back to the terrace steps, still keeping within the shadow of the hedge, and yet get her head to a level where she could see inside the lighted room, might it not be worth the risk?

She was on her back now, and with her elbows and heels she moved her body out from under the hedge to the dew-laden grass. She sat up, leaned forward, and got to her knees. Inch by inch, crawling softly along, she came to the steps. The lower ones were in the shadow of the oak, but the top one was bathed in light. She would have to be very cautious indeed.

Stiffly she got to a crouching position, then, keeping well in the shadow, stood up. The scene inside the room was as clear as though she had been seeing it on a motion-picture screen.

8

THE ROOM INTO WHICH JUDY PEERED was obviously the library. Paneled in dark wood, it had a stone fireplace on the far wall with bookcases built in at either side. A couch was set at right angles to the hearth, and a couple of deep leather chairs were pulled close to a small table holding a decanter and two tall glasses. But the furnishings were completely lost on Judy. She was interested in the occupants. And what she saw made her crane her neck and take an involuntary step closer.

On a card table placed almost directly in front of the door Mr. Gross was holding a black cocker spaniel. His right hand cupped the dog's chin, his left forefinger and thumb held the tassel of the cut tail, and he was looking from the dog to a thin, beak-nosed man who was talking in a voice pitched so low that it carried to Judy only as a wordless rumble.

The scene was not without action. Every now and then Mr. Gross abandoned his hold on the tail to place his hand under the dog's body and raise and lower it with a jouncing motion, as though he were trying to arrange a more perfect stance. The beak-nosed man would cock his head and back away, or squat on the floor to look up at the dog with sharp, interested eyes.

Since the stranger was facing her, Judy could see his every motion. He was obviously giving his opinion of the spaniel on the table. But whether the cocker under consideration was either Shadow, Sambo, or some other black dog from Mr. Gross's large kennels, Judy could not possibly be sure. Under the strong light, seen from without, the animal was in unrelieved silhouette. He looked more like a growing puppy than an adult dog, because he was small and the feathers on his legs didn't seem very long, seen as they were in outline.

Spellbound, Judy watched the pantomime for several minutes. Then she jumped as she heard Mr. Gross whistle sharply and at the same time release his hold on the dog. The pup leaped from the table to the floor with an easy, graceful motion as the fat man bent to lift a second spaniel, identical to the first, with a single, scooping motion of his thick-fingered hand.

Judy almost gasped aloud. This couldn't be coincidence. No two other pups, even in silhouette, could possibly look so much alike! These *must* be Shadow and Sambo the two men were discussing. If only, only, only she could hear their words!

As the routine she had watched before was repeated with this second dog Judy considered how she might get closer. She dared not sneak up the terrace steps directly into the beam of light, yet the thick barberry hedge which surrounded the rest of the terrace was as great a protection against intruders as a barbed-wire fence. There was no help for it. She was stymied. She could see but not hear a word of what passed between the two men.

The worst of it was that Judy had a hunch this conversation might be important. The half hour, she knew, must be nearly up, and instead of standing in this shadow, trying to catch a single word which might emerge from the rumble of the beak-nosed man's voice, she should have been making tracks back to the road and Jeff. Still she hesitated. Still she waited, daring her luck a second time, hoping for—what?

The man called Fitz seemed to have finished his monologue. He ruffled the hair on the spaniel's head with a roughly affectionate hand, then walked over to the small table and lighted a cigarette. The two cockers jumped to the couch and curled up in a single ball, and Judy dodged again beneath the barberry as the men walked to the terrace door and stepped calmly out.

For Judy, the peak of terror had been reached. It couldn't be repeated. She was astonished at her own calmness as she lay motionless under the hedge and listened to a conversation which was now very plain. As long as Mr. Gross didn't let the puppies out to go sniffing around and searching out her scent she felt that she was comparatively safe.

Clop, clop, clop went two pairs of shoes on the stone floor, punctuating their wearers' words.

"Then you're pretty darned sure they'll be big-time stuff," said Gross.

"Not a question of a doubt," came the reply of the man called Fitz. "If I've ever picked a winner you've got one there." He chuckled. "Or rather two."

The men must have paused at the far side of the terrace, because Judy, though she strained her ears to hear, lost Mr. Gross's next remark. Then she heard their footsteps turn and start back, and she heard the kennel owner say, "Of course they're young yet."

"Too young to decide between," Fitz agreed. "Let me see them again in three or four months."

"That'd be very decent of you, Fitz."

"Not at all. I'm interested. You've done a remarkable job, Mr. Gross. Remarkable! I saw My Own Brucie as a pup, and not even he could top them."

"That's what I want to hear!" Mr. Gross sounded very much set up. He positively chuckled with pleasure.

"Keep one and sell one," suggested Fitz. "That's my advice. At a year either of those dogs will bring a cool thousand."

"I'm not interested in the money, Fitzhugh," said Mr. Gross rather testily. "You know that." Then a smug quality crept into his voice as he continued. "I'm simply interested in improving the breed . . ."

Judy heard the door creak open, then shut, as the last part of the sentence faded. She took a long breath, counted to ten, then dared to peek out from her hiding place. Mr. Gross was on the far side of the library with the decanter in his hand and his guest was crushing out a cigarette. Now, if ever, was the time to be on her way.

She gave one hasty glance around, but the garden seemed quiet and empty. Softly she crept back along the bristling hedge to the drive, which shone unbrokenly in the moonlight. Moving like a cat, she slipped across. Once in the shelter of the long row of trees she felt more secure. She stopped to slip into her loafers, then sped like a gazelle toward the great iron gate, no longer caring much that an occasional twig cracked beneath her flying feet.

As she ran, she wondered whether Jeff had already passed Gross Point on his way to the Thomas house. The concentration with which she had listened to the conversation on the terrace had destroyed her sense of time. But as she drew near the road she heard her twin's familiar whistle, and she raced between the gateposts to land almost in his arms.

"Judy, what on earth . . ."

Breathless, she took his hand and turned him toward home, urging him down the hill. "I'll tell you later. Just now, let's run!"

She wanted, with an urge that was childish but irresistible, to put all the distance she could between herself and Gross Point before she stopped to talk. Usually the faster runner of the two, Jeff was hard put to keep up with her. But at last Judy stopped, panting, by the old stone bridge which spanned the creek. She sat on the low coping and swung her long legs over the side. Now, within shouting distance of her own home, she again felt perfectly safe.

There she finally gasped out the whole astonishing story to Jeff.

The boy's reactions varied. When Judy described her first impulsive desire to get to the dogs, Jeff looked at her as though she were crazy. While half admiring her daring, he ridiculed her attempt to reach the kennels. "You're a mutt!" he scolded. "Don't you know every last dog in those runs would set up a barking to wake the dead if a stranger approached at night?"

"I found that out," Judy admitted. "But at the time I didn't think."

"You *deserved* to be caught."

"I wasn't though!" Judy bridled. "Now sh! Let me go on."

When she came to the part about the conversation she slowed down, trying to remember exactly the words that had passed between the two men. Jeff listened intently, then made her repeat what she had said. Judy was sure of her ground. She told the story the same way twice.

When she finished, Jeff gave a low, surprised whistle, and shook his head thoughtfully.

"A thousand dollars!" Judy breathed, trying to picture such a large amount of money all in dollar bills. "Do you suppose any dog in the world could really be worth that?"

But Jeff wasn't whistling at the price put on the spaniels. Judy's narrative seemed to knock neatly in the head a theory on which he'd been working. "I'm not interested in the money," Gross had said, "I'm simply interested in improving the breed." If money were no object, if Mr. Gross could buy any dog he fancied, wasn't it absurd to imagine that he might have stolen Lynn's pups?

"Do you, Jeff?" Judy was repeating.

"Do I what?"

"Suppose any dog is worth that much money?"

"I don't know anything about what show dogs sell for," Jeff replied. "But a thousand bucks sounds like a lot."

"Sounds! It *is* a lot," Judy insisted. "It would be a reason, wouldn't it, why Mr. Matthews would be enough upset by the loss of his pups to come down and see Dad."

"Yeah, sure," Jeff frowned. "But how would a

gardener get two pups worth that kind of money in the first place? Nobody's giving away two thousand berries these days."

"Did he say they were a gift?"

"I don't know. But everybody's been saying a lot. Lynn says Gross's pups are hers, but Gross says they're his. I suppose the stork must've brought the ones that are up at Matthews' now. Everybody talks so much you don't know who to believe."

"I believe Lynn, Jeff Sutherland, and you do too. You know it!"

"All right, all right. But the fact remains that Gross has registration papers and Lynn hasn't. It'll take more than believing in Lynn to crack this thing open. It'll take some really thorough work."

Judy reached down and touched her legs gently where the barberry had cut them. She was beginning to feel she'd like to get home and put some witch hazel on the scratches. "Like what?" she asked.

"Like this. I think that all along we've been going at this thing backward. While you were baby sitting tonight I was reading that Sherlock Holmes book of Dad's. Now there was a guy who used his bean. He didn't play guessing games. He got all the facts of the case lined up and didn't go skipping off on the trail of haphazard clues."

Judy felt that the discussion was getting rather academic, and her scratches, now that the exhilaration of her adventure had worn off, were getting more and more painful. She swung her legs over the coping and eased herself carefully to the ground. "Come on," she said. "Let's go home. We can talk on the way."

It was Jeff who did the talking. He outlined two or three of Conan Doyle's thrilling mysteries in which his hero, Mr. Holmes, used his almost uncanny talents to great advantage. "You see?" he said.

Judy didn't see. She wasn't even listening very carefully. She was thinking about how her legs hurt, and wondering what under the sun she'd ever tell mother to explain the state of her dress.

But again Judy was lucky. When she and Jeff reached home the living room lights had been turned off and only the hall lantern left burning. Voices came from behind the door of the master bedroom, and it was no trick at all for Judy to get to her own room without being seen.

Jeff came into the bathroom and continued his monologue about Sherlock Holmes while Judy dabbed at her cuts. He helped her to inspect the damage to the dress, which was really not so bad, after all. It was stained with grass and earth, from rolling under the hedge, but the barberry had scarcely pricked it. With a pin Judy pulled through the few threads that had been caught up by the thorns and which lay in telltale loops on the right side.

"Put it in the laundry basket and forget about it," Jeff advised.

Judy did just that. She got into her pajamas and

brushed the scraps of dead leaves out of her hair, sitting in front of her full-skirted dressing table and feeling rather let down. Jeff and his Sherlock Holmes! This had been *her* evening—*her* adventure! She wanted to talk about Gross Point, to go over and over the implications of what she had seen and heard. And what did Jeff do! He switched the subject, first chance he got, to this guy Holmes.

Her brother came into her room just then to describe another phase of Holmes's technique which he'd forgotten to mention.

"Sure," said Judy, brushing her hair with added vigor. "So what? That's all storybook stuff. What I'd like to know is this: What are we going to do about Lynn and her spaniels?"

Jeff, who wasn't in the least sleepy, threw himself across Judy's bed. "I was getting to that," he said. "It seems to me we ought to take one thing at a time and the most important thing first."

"What's the most important thing?"

Jeff leaned on his elbows and held the crown of his head in his hands, the short hair of his crew cut bristling up between his fingers. He stared down at the bedspread and looked very thoughtful. "I think it's this," he finally decided. "Did anybody give Lynn or her father two black puppies?"

"But Lynn *said*—"

"Lynn said she couldn't tell where she got them. But we've got to find out. It shouldn't be hard. We ought to talk to all the people Mr. Matthews works for. We ought to find out about his job at Carstairs' Castle. Remember, Judy, Mr. Gross has perfectly authentic registration papers on those dogs, and unless we have some really neat evidence to go on, we'll never get them away from him now!"

Judy admitted Jeff's logic, but his method sounded painstaking and slow. She immediately began to put up objections. "We don't even know what people Mr. Matthews works for. And if we did we might run into him at some house, and then what would we say? Carstairs' Castle is all closed up. Daddy said so. Anyway, all that would take *forever!*" she ended feebly.

Jeff saw Judy's "forever" as a matter of weeks, and said so, undismayed. "We've got to find out," he insisted. "We'll start tomorrow morning."

IT WAS JUST AS
Judy had said. In a book
nothing would have in-
terfered with their plans to begin their detective work
the very next morning, but in real life a dozen things
made it impossible to do what she and Jeff had ar-
ranged.

To begin with, it turned unbearably hot. Mrs.
Sutherland wilted by midmorning, acquired what she
always called a "splitting" headache, and kept the
twins at home, helping with this and that, until noon.
Mamam's train was due to pull in at 12:38, and she
really didn't feel up to meeting it, though she thought
she must.

Sitting down on a chair in the entrance hall, she felt
very ill. She passed her hand over her damp forehead
and said, "Poor Mamam, traveling in this heat!" It
wasn't that she had so far to come—just from Camden, across the Delaware from Philadelphia—but she
was such an elderly lady to be attempting the station
steps and the train stairs alone.

Jeff always felt helpless when his mother wasn't

well. He stood leaning against the doorjamb, trying to smooth off a broken fingernail with his Scout knife, scowling angrily, and not knowing what to do.

Judy was more resourceful. "Why don't Jeff and I ride down on our bikes and meet Mamam's train?" she suggested. "We could put her in a taxi and convoy her home."

"But it's so *hot!*" Mrs. Sutherland protested weakly.

"Phooey, we don't mind the heat," Jeff chimed in.

"And while we're gone you could take some aspirin and get a nap," added Judy. She was thinking that she'd certainly rather ride her bike in to Wayne than be drafted for any more housework. It was fairly obvious that no extensive sleuthing could be done that day, but even so she felt that it might further their mutual cause to be with Jeff, alone. Then if either of them had a bright idea about the cocker spaniel mystery they could at least talk about it.

But when it actually came to the point they had little to say. They rode in to Wayne under the scorching sun in almost complete silence, saving their breath for the uphill climbs, and when they arrived in the comparative shelter of the station platform there were only five minutes to go before the 12:38 pulled in.

For some reason, on that boiling day, the noon train was crowded. It was some seconds before they recognized Mamam, a slight little figure in stiff, prewar black taffeta, rustling down the platform with an outmoded bonnet cocked rakishly on her head.

"Well, children," she said briskly in a voice thin with age, "how are you?" She pecked each in turn on the right cheek, handed Jeff her battered suitcase, and marched ahead of them to the uneven and risky cement stairs.

Judy hurried up and offered her arm, but Mamam refused it. "I've got along good enough for eighty-one years. I guess I can manage a year or two more." But her eyes twinkled so brightly at Judy that her words held no offense.

On the ground level, because Mamam's descent had been rather slow despite her lack of caution, the only two available taxis were gone. Jeff felt badly because he'd neglected to reserve one, but Mamam seemed unperturbed. "They won't be long," she said calmly. "We'll just wait. When you get to be my age a few minutes one way or the other don't matter a hip-hip-hooray."

"But it's so *hot!*" Judy protested.

"Hot?" With the thermometer quivering at 97 in the shade Mamam made it a question. "You children don't know anything about heat. If you'd lived through the summer of '83 . . ."

Neither Jeff nor Judy heard the finish of this remark. Into the parking area was pulling a station wagon with maroon trim, as polished as though it had just emerged from a showcase. On the door, in maroon and gold letters, was painted, "Artemus Gross," and beneath it, "Gross Point Kennels."

Judy had a queer, sinking sensation in her stomach. She had no wish to run into Mr. Gross again. Besides the remembrance of their last encounter she had on her conscience her eavesdropping of the night before. But the man at the driver's seat, fortunately, was not the master of Gross Point. This man was gaunt, with high cheekbones and thick black hair. He was dressed in old breeches and a brown checked shirt, a costume which tagged him at once in the minds of the twins as the new kennelman.

The wagon, as it happened, pulled up at the curb almost immediately in front of where the twins and Mamam were standing. Even Mamam, with her fading eyesight, could read the legend on the door.

"Artemus Gross," she piped up. "Well, I'll be!"

Judy and Jeff both looked at her. "D'you know him?" they asked at once.

Mamam nodded her head rapidly. "'Course," she replied. "'Course." The children had evidently forgotten that she knew practically everybody who was anybody in this slice of the world, except for upstarts who had migrated to Philadelphia within the last generation. "Used to live on State Street not far from us. Not far from the Curtises either. Many's the time I've seen Ella Gross scrubbing down her own marble steps." She glanced again at the station wagon. "Guess they're pretty uppity now."

The twins were listening to Mamam and watching what went on at the station wagon at the same time.

The kennelman, if kennelman he was, had lowered the back of the wagon and was lifting out a heavy, slatted crate from which there came the petulant barking of a dog. On several of the slats were painted large black letters spelling the address to which the dog was evidently to be shipped. Through the openings Judy could see an occasional flash of red and white fur. She heaved a sigh of relief. At least the box didn't contain either of the black pups.

Mamam was continuing her monologue. She was always good for ten minutes, once started. "Let me see—it must be Young Art who owns that contraption. Old Art's been dead nigh onto ten years. Good riddance too. He was a scoundrel if I ever saw one."

Mamam had never been one to stifle her likes and dislikes, but the ringing tone in which she delivered this denunciation embarrassed Jeff. "Sh! That man'll hear you," he warned, wishing the taxi would hurry back so that they could get Mamam on her way.

"What if he does?" bridled Mamam, nevertheless lowering her voice. "Everybody in Camden'd say the same thing."

Camden was still the center of Mamam's world, even though almost everyone who could claim fame or fortune had moved to the other side of the river. She remembered Walt Whitman, the poet, and Cyrus Curtis, founder of *The Saturday Evening Post,* and she talked about these personages familiarly, as though they were in the habit of running over to borrow an egg or two, mornings. She talked about Artemus Gross, Sr., in that way now. But she broke off suddenly when the crate slapped to the ground and the dog let out a frightened yelp.

"What's he got in there?" she asked sharply. "A dog, is it? What's he doing with it?"

Before either of the twins had the presence of mind to stop her, she walked jerkily over to the rear of the wagon and tapped the kennelman on the shoulder with the cane she had lately consented to carry.

"Young man, what are you doing with that dog?"

The man, who was anything but young, turned, startled. Seeing a very elderly lady, he raised one hand to his forehead as though he wanted to tip his hat. It probably never occurred to him that the question was none of Mamam's business. "We're shippin' her out, ma'am," he said promptly. "To Brattleboro, Vermont, for breedin' purposes."

Mamam peered into the crate. "Is she comfortable?"

"As comfortable as possible, ma'am."

"Has she water?"

"The fella in the baggage car'll take care of that."

"Well, see that he does," said Mamam sharply. "Sending a scared little dog all the way to Vermont seems a senseless thing to do, but then Young Art Gross never did care much about other people's feelings and I suppose that carries right on through to animals. Why, I remember . . ."

"Mamam, here's the taxi!" Just what Mamam remembered the kennelman was never to know, and it was with great relief that the twins saw her safely on her way out of the station yard. They mounted their bikes and pedaled rapidly after the cab, putting a full square between themselves and the station wagon before they relaxed and burst into laughter.

"I'd like to see her handle Young Art in person," Judy giggled. "I think she'd be a match for him."

"When we get a chance," suggested Jeff, "let's tell her about the mystery. She'd get a big wallop out of it. And," he added thoughtfully, "she might even be of some help."

When the twins reached home their mother was up and dressed, her headache much better. Mamam was ensconced in a Cape Cod rocker, tatting for all she was worth, while she kept up a running monologue designed to bring Mrs. Sutherland up to date on a great many things of local importance. They all lunched on sandwiches and tall glasses of chocolate milk, after which the twins persuaded their mother that the only sensible course on such a beastly day was to make ice cream for dinner.

Jeff, at least, pushed this idea with forethought. Whenever his mother made a frozen dessert she usually needed extra cream, and the quickest and richest source of supply was the Matthews' cow.

"If you want a pint of cream from Matthews' I'll walk up and get it," he offered generously.

"O Jeff, but it's so hot to climb that hill," his mother demurred, then said in the next breath, "See if there's forty cents in my pocketbook."

Judy, who was indefatigable, volunteered to accompany her brother, and set out, much against the better judgment of Mamam, who considered that the proper place for a young girl on a blistering summer afternoon was in the house with the shades drawn.

Judy began to think so too by the time she reached the top of the hill. Even in a thin Antibes shirt and shorts she was streaming with perspiration. "The cream'll turn sour before we get it home," she warned, mopping her neck with a damp handkerchief.

But Jeff wasn't thinking about cream. He was wondering how adroitly he could persuade Lynn to tell him the names of some of her father's present employers. As he explained to Judy, he didn't think it would be smart to ask her outright. It would look awfully nosy; she might even think they were trying to put Mr. Matthews in a spot.

The flimsy frame house, when they reached it, lay

inert under the sun. No sign of activity greeted their coming. The dogs didn't bark. Even the chickens were sleepy and still. But Lynn answered Judy's light knock at once. She looked gaunt, tired, and worried in the strong light from the doorway. "Hello," she said.

"Hello," replied Judy. "Mother wondered if you could sell us some cream."

"I guess so," Lynn answered apathetically. She hesitated a moment, then added, "Will you come in?"

"You just bet!" Jeff replied for both of them. "It's hot as blazes out here. I'd like to beg a drink of water too."

The room which they entered was threadbare but clean. Neither Jeff nor Judy had ever before been in the Matthews' house and they were both shocked by its ugliness. A black mission armchair rubbed elbows with a golden-oak table. A sagging upholstered couch, boasting no slip cover, was covered in moth-eaten frieze, which looked uninviting and prickly. No books relieved the dullness of the room, and a wilting bunch of flowers in an old blue bowl was the one attempt at color. While Lynn went back to the kitchen for Jeff's glass of water Judy's eyes wandered from the patterned congoleum rug to the curtainless windows. Somebody ought to show Lynn what to do with this place. Why, with a can of paint and a few yards of fabric . . .

Lynn came back from the kitchen with a pitcher of water and glasses. She was accompanied by two bounding puppies, panting from the heat but exuberant at the chance to investigate the guests. Judy smiled and dropped at once to her knees, gathering the soft, struggling bodies to her. "I'd settle for these two wild Indians any day!" she laughed.

Something in this remark made Lynn stiffen. Perhaps she imagined that Judy was trying to say, in a backhanded way, that she should stop mourning for the dogs they all thought of as Shadow and Sambo, and be happy with what she had in hand.

In any event, every attempt that Jeff made to draw the girl out on the subject of her father's occupation died a quick death. She was polite but distant. She answered direct questions but seemed to want to avoid the subject which most concerned her. After a few minutes she excused herself to go back to the spring-house and ladle out the pint of cream, and when she returned she did not sit down again, which seemed a pretty plain indication to Jeff that she expected Judy and him to go.

On the way home Jeff was disgruntled. "It was your bright remark about the dogs that threw her off," he complained to his twin.

"I don't care," Judy snapped back, dripping and uncomfortable. "They *are* sweet pups. Any girl in the world'd be glad to own them."

"Except Lynn Matthews," replied Jeff.

By bedtime, however, the twins were reconciled. Judy, with an electric fan trained on the floor, was lying full length on a rag rug enjoying the novelty of her hair whipping in its breeze. She was fresh from a bath and feeling very friendly, so she smiled brightly up at Jeff when he appeared in the doorway.

"I've been thinking," he said solemnly.

"No!"

Jeff ignored this pert remark. "We've got to start somewhere," he went on, "so it may as well be with Carstairs' Castle."

Judy rolled over and sat up, hugging her knees. This sounded like fun! "Do you know where it is?" she asked.

"Just about. I got that large-scale map of Dad's out of the car and I'm pretty sure it's out near King of Prussia Road, about two miles from here."

"Let's go tomorrow!"

"That's what I was thinking."

"Rain or shine?"

"Come what may," replied Jeff firmly.

And Judy echoed it. "Come what may."

What came was a brief midnight thunderstorm which did little to cool the atmosphere but which invited a low-lying fog that clung to the hills surrounding the Sutherlands' house long after the breakfast dishes were washed.

"It looks like clam broth," complained Judy, peering out, but Jeff pointed hopefully to a feeble circle of light in the eastern sky which he insisted was the sun.

"We said, 'Come what way,' " he reminded Judy, and, not to be outdone, his twin came back with, "All right, let's go."

It was eerie riding through the fog, which trailed long scarves of mist against their legs and across their faces. Mrs. Sutherland had been persuaded, reluctantly, to pack them a picnic lunch, which Jeff carried in his bicycle basket. He insisted that every few seconds they should clang their bells, to avoid a possible collision with an oncoming car.

Cautiously they proceeded from landmark to familiar landmark. When they climbed to the top of a hill they would stand for a few moments in feeble, curtained sunlight to look down on the gray blanket which shrouded the next valley. Then down into the fog they would swoop, the repeated b-b-b-ring of their bicycle bells warning all and sundry who might be in their paths.

Finally they came to a road sign from which Jeff took his bearings and led them off into unfamiliar territory. The fences and gateposts were no longer ones they recognized, and Judy felt like an explorer in an uncharted land. It made her shiver a little to fly past the strange shapes that rose out of the mist, and she was reminded of all the fairy stories she had ever read, of hobgoblins and genii who peopled moist and dripping woods, of trees whose branches reached out like arms to clutch the unsuspecting wayfarer.

Jeff stopped at another crossroads and Judy, engrossed in her private game of imagination, almost piled into him. "I think we go right," he said.

"What I want to know," put in Judy, "is how we're ever going to find our way back."

"Oh, that'll be easy," Jeff insisted. "The fog will have lifted by noon."

It didn't look to Judy as though the fog would ever lift. It seemed much too clinging to be flung off— poof!—by a remark of Jeff's. Yet she rather liked the quality of unreality the mist lent to their excursion. It made everything seem properly mysterious.

She said as much to Jeff, but her twin was busy peering through the fog. "Watch for a long fence on the left, then a gatehouse, then a high hedge. The hedge ought to border the Carstairs place if Bill Rogers is right."

"Bill Rogers?"

"He was talking about a fishpond he'd heard about at Carstairs' Castle and wondering if it was still stocked."

"Oh, I see," said Judy. "I was wondering how just a road map could be so much help."

"I don't tell you *everything*," Jeff flashed back. "Look, here's the fence."

"And the gatehouse," Judy said a few minutes later. "Then this ought to be the hedge." Her eyes rose to where the top of the privet was lost in the fog. "It would be unclipped, I suppose."

Jeff, ahead, had paused at the place where a rutted

drive led off the road. No gate marked the entrance to Carstairs' Castle, just a tangle of shrubbery that spilled out of the mist to surround a rotting post topped by a rusty wrought-iron lamp. "I'm pretty sure this is it."

Judy said: "We'd better walk our bikes. This road looks bad."

They went up the drive side by side, weeds and grass tickling their legs. Both of them were remembering the last time they had trespassed, uninvited, on another person's property, and both half expected to see an irate caretaker pop out of the fog to order them to be gone. But only the chirping of birds and the crunch of their shoes and the bicycle wheels against the gravel disturbed the peace.

The drive ran straight for several hundred yards, then curved abruptly to the left. The sun, high enough by now to make the mist defenseless, showed the twins another abrupt turn to the right, down a short hill and across a bridge to a saucerlike valley, in the center of which, surrounded by weeping willows, stood a crumbling Victorian mansion with a mansard roof, lifting gloomy stone towers to the sky.

Before the house the drive circled an enormous iron vase, empty now of flowers, and ran under a porte-cochere from which broad steps led to a balustraded porch. Encouraged by the emerging sun, Judy and Jeff rode rapidly down the hill and swept around the turn to lean their bikes against the steps.

"Any minute now," whispered Judy, "a lady in a bustle will walk out that door."

Jeff glanced at the carved-wood door in spite of himself, but his attention was really on the lawn. "Imagine," he said, "trying to take care of a place like this on one day a week!"

This brought Judy's attention back to Mr. Matthews, and the real object of their visit. Now that they were here, she wondered what they had really expected to find. Certainly this abandoned Victorian castle seemed to shed no light on the black spaniel mystery. Probably the most sensible thing to do was to write it off as a fruitless quest and sit right down on these steps and eat an early lunch. She eyed the package in Jeff's bicycle basket hungrily.

But her twin had other ideas. He was already walking around to the rear of the house, as though he were looking for something. Judy shrugged and trailed after him.

"Jeff," she began, "don't you think it would be a good idea to eat . . ." Then her eye was unexpectedly caught by the broken pane of a side window. Like a flash her enthusiasm revived. "Hey! Jeff! Look!" Even before her twin could turn back Judy was feeling cautiously for the latch which she could just barely reach inside.

10

JUDY STEPPED OVER THE LOW WINDOW
sill into a dim Victorian parlor, where furniture
writhed and twisted in somber patterns of dark wood.
Upholstered pieces, swathed in dust covers, crouched
like fat ghosts, and sober farm animals, captured for
eternity in oil paint, stared down at the twins from
within ornate gilt frames. Jeff, just behind his sister,
whistled softly, "Golly," he said in a hushed voice,
"no wonder they call it Carstairs' Castle."

Judy stood with her hands clasped. She had forgotten, for the moment, the mystery that had brought
them here, and she was seeing the parlor as it must
once have been, cluttered with antimacassars, plush
albums, and whatnots, a perfect setting for a thin Victorian lady with a velvet ribbon encircling her white
neck. "You could write a book about a house like
this," she sighed.

"*You* write it," suggested Jeff, who hated English composition. "I'm going to have a look around."

"Oh, do you think we ought?" Judy asked without really meaning it, and her twin looked over his shoulder at her in astonishment.

"Are you kidding? Who got us in here, I'd like to know?"

Judy had the grace to blush. She'd only made the remark to satisfy a vague instinct toward the amenities which the house had put upon her. Actually, she was as eager as Jeff to explore.

Walking softly, they went from the parlor to a wide entrance hall. Here there was no rug on the floor and great squares on the wall showed that many pictures had been removed. Double doors led into a dining room, and creaked sternly as Jeff pushed them open. An enormous Empire buffet filled one wall and a long table occupied the center of the room, but there were no chairs at all.

"Looks like they've sold a lot of stuff," Jeff remarked.

"They? I thought Miss Carstairs lived here all alone." Judy shivered slightly at the thought, for the house had obviously been furnished in a decade of ugliness. As she and Jeff tiptoed from room to dim room, their eyes becoming gradually accustomed to the light that filtered through cracks in the drawn shades, she became increasingly glad that she herself had been born in an age of white paint and gay furnishings. "Imagine staying here by yourself!"

"Oh, I don't know—maybe she liked it." There was a faded elegance to the place that impressed Jeff. He didn't share Judy's need for bright, warm surroundings. "Shall we go upstairs?"

"Let's!"

The stairs were still carpeted in dark red, with brass rods on each step. A stained-glass window decorated the landing, barely lighting the long upstairs hall, from which opened a series of doors. To look into one bedroom was to see them all. Carved headboards reared above hair-mattressed beds, now denuded of coverlets. White or brown marble topped the bureaus. Few ornaments were left about, and the rooms looked cold and forlorn, even in midsummer.

Only when they reached the end of the hall did Judy and Jeff come on an apartment different from the rest. They opened a final door upon a suite of two rooms, a bedroom and a sitting room. Here the wallpaper, sprigged with rosebuds, was still quite fresh. Most of the bedroom furniture had been removed, but the sitting room was almost intact. There were low rockers, a footstool, a round table, a chaise longue, and a lady's small writing desk. One shade had shot to the very top, flooding the small room with sunlight, and on the desk, as though they had been sorted through and discarded, lay a sheaf of papers.

Judy walked over and glanced down at them curiously, then riffled through them with one hand. She caught herself wondering if detectives ever had a similarly guilty feeling at going through another person's desk. There wasn't much here anyway—gas and telephone bills, a couple of invitations, a letter beginning, "Dear Ellen," which broke off after a few innocuous sentences. Miss Carstairs had apparently left little of her personal life behind.

Automatically Judy straightened the worn blotter, and as she did so the yellowed corner of an old snapshot, tucked under the pad and forgotten, met her fingers. She drew it out, not noticing that a companion to it fluttered to the floor. Judy saw a picture of a Gibson girl with an enormous pompadour and a tiny waist, holding a businesslike tennis racket in one fragile hand. She smiled and turned to Jeff. "Look," she said. "Imagine playing tennis in this outfit!"

But Jeff was bending down to pick up the other snapshot, in which a middle-aged woman, seated on a stone garden bench, was holding a handsome parti-colored cocker spaniel.

"Look at *this!*" Jeff said.

Judy looked. "That's a pretty dog, isn't it?" she said, but she thought it was silly of Jeff to attach special significance to the print. "Don't get *too* cocker-conscious," she warned him. "You'll be seeing them behind every bush."

But Jeff was examining the snapshot closely. "That's more than a pretty dog," he insisted. "That's a humdinger. I wonder if the old gal is Miss Carstairs?" He turned the photo over. On the back, in fading ink, was written, "Amelia and Gay Lady."

Hopefully, then, the twins began to make a systematic search of the desk. The two top drawers were empty, but the bottom one held a stack of old photos, taken at the beach, in the mountains, and on the grounds of Carstairs' Castle. There was nothing of special interest to Jeff, however, until he came to a folder, near the bottom of the stack, which was crisp with its fifteen years of age and which announced the entries in the Philadelphia Dog Show. Jeff took it to the window and searched through it for the spaniel listings. Finally he found what he wanted—a reference to Carstairs' Gay Lady, handled by a certain John Cloud and owned by Miss Amelia Carstairs.

"You see!" he crowed. "Miss Carstairs was interested in cockers."

But Judy scoffed. "Fifteen years ago. So what? I can't see what you're driving at."

Jeff didn't quite

know himself, but he went through the rest of the house inattentively, his mind searching for some connection. He was still wandering in his private fog when Judy began to think about lunch again. Her stomach felt like a yawning cavern, and she said abruptly, "Let's eat!"

They raced each other to the open parlor window and stepped from the musty gloom of the house into sunshine which was now warm and bright. The sandwiches and fruit tasted wonderful to Judy, but Jeff munched his share absentmindedly, leaning back against a pillar of the porch and looking off over the uncut grass to the background plantings of trees and shrubs.

Finally he sat up. "I'm going around back," he announced. "While we're here we might as well see all there is to see."

Judy shrugged and trailed after him. For her part, she thought the approved detective technique was vastly overrated. She'd rather hoped to find a clue in every room of Carstairs' Castle, and what had they come out with—an ancient dog-show program and an equally ancient picture of a dog that must now be dead. Why Jeff, usually practical to a fault, should get so excited—well, Judy just didn't know.

At the rear of the house the lawn dropped to a small pond, possibly stocked with the fish in which Bill Rogers, Jeff's friend, had been interested. Off to the right was an abandoned kitchen garden and a low frame structure with its roof bashed in. Jeff ignored the fishpond, curiously, and hurried in the direction of the frame building which looked to Judy like a chicken house. "Come here," he called.

Judy sauntered over. "No, thanks, I don't want any eggs," she said.

"Eggs!" Jeff snorted, ignoring the attempt at a joke. "Use your eyes, Judy Sutherland. This was never a chicken coop. This was a kennel. See those sagging strips of wire. They fenced in runs."

Judy looked more closely. Jeff might be right, she conceded. Weeds grew so high that she couldn't be sure, but she was willing to give her twin the benefit of the doubt. "If they did," she murmured, "they fenced them in a doggone long time ago. See that tree?"

Jeff's eyes followed his twin's to a fair-sized maple, standing at least twenty feet high, which grew just within the inclosure. Judy was right. No dogs had been kept here for a good many years. It was going to be hard to tie up today's discoveries with two pairs of five-month-old pups. "Yeah, I guess you're right," he admitted, and wandered dejectedly on down to the pond, managing to spot a couple of small fish, which raised his spirits slightly.

Judy was in a mood to kid him. "Do those fish lead you to suspect a large man with red hair?" she asked. As far as she was concerned this game was over. The sun was getting really hot now, and it would be a sticky ride home. "Come on. Let's go," she suggested, stepping cautiously back through a patch of weeds with a weather eye out for poison ivy.

Jeff consented agreeably enough. They mounted their bikes and jounced along the drive to a point where the rising ground forced them to get off and push. At the turn they looked back on Carstairs' Castle, less interesting under the glare of noon than it had been in the morning mist. It no longer looked romantic. Instead, it looked old and decaying and ugly.

> " 'Things are seldom what they seem;
>   Skim milk masquerades as cream. . . .' "

Judy sang the words from *Pinafore* ruefully, thinking for the first time that Gilbert and Sullivan contained a lot of common sense.

They rode, without saying much, to the crossroads which led in one direction toward home, in the other toward Wayne. Then Jeff said, "Want to ride into town and get a milk shake?"

Judy felt brighter at once. "D'you have any money?"

"Fifty cents. I'll *loan* you some." Jeff wanted to get the business arrangements on a firm footing.

"Till next week?"

Jeff considered. A milk shake would taste awfully good. "O.K.," he agreed.

Fifteen minutes later the twins were perched securely on the high stools of the small drugstore which served the largest milk shakes in Wayne. It wasn't a chain store, like many. It had been owned by one man for a long, long time and he served Judy and Jeff himself, since the high-school boy who had the soda-jerking job for the summer was off on his lunch hour.

Jeff leaned his elbows on the counter as the druggist stirred the chocolate up from the bottom of the built-in container with a long, thin-handled spoon. "Mr. Jones," Judy was surprised to hear him say, "did you ever know Miss Carstairs well?"

"Miss Amelia? Sure. Every shopkeeper my age in town knew Miss Carstairs. Miss her too."

"When did she move away?" Jeff asked.

The druggist shrugged. "Early spring. Maybe March. Why?"

"I was just wondering if I could get permission to fish in her pond, that's all," Judy heard Jeff say glibly. "D'you know where she's living?"

"With her younger sister, I think. The married one. Out West somewhere, it seems to me."

Something stirred in Judy's brain, but Jeff's next words commanded her attention.

"Mr. Jones, did Miss Amelia Carstairs ever breed dogs?"

"You bet. Cockers. Fine ones too. Not many, but good." Mr. Jones broke off and looked at Jeff quizzically. "What's that got to do with fishing?"

Judy wished she could say, "That's another kind of

fishing." Why did she always think of bright remarks when they couldn't be used?

"Nothing," Jeff grinned back at Mr. Jones. "Saw a picture once of a dog called 'Gay Lady.' I was just wondering, that's all."

The explanation seemed to satisfy Mr. Jones. There were no other customers in the store, and he was not disinclined to gossip. Few youngsters who came in ever urged him to talk about old times.

"Gay Lady was a show dog," he said. "The first big winner Miss Amelia ever had. That was when there was money in that family, and Carstairs' Castle was still quite a place, for all its old-fashioned, gingerbread architecture. Miss Amelia's father built the house, you know."

Jeff didn't know, nor did he very much care. He was interested in talking about dogs, and he steered the conversation back as adroitly as he could.

"The man Miss Amelia was engaged to gave her Gay Lady," Mr. Jones said with a sigh. "Fine gentleman he was too, even if he did come from New York. Killed in a railroad accident. Pity. Miss Amelia never took a shine to anybody else, I guess."

"Did Gay Lady start her off on breeding dogs?" Jeff wasn't in the least interested in a forgotten love affair.

"Yep. That's it. She didn't do it for profit, you understand. Just to improve the breed."

Judy glanced at her twin. She'd heard that one

before. But Jeff was watching Mr. Jones, who was wiping his eyeglasses and continuing.

"I remember one day she walked in here and told me she aimed to breed the finest cockers east of the Mississippi. 'That's a pretty large order, Miss Amelia,' I said, and she said, 'I know it is, Mr. Jones, but with patience it can be done, and I've got plenty of patience.' Poor soul, I guess she meant she didn't have much else, except money, and after her pa died she didn't even have that."

"Was that when she stopped breeding dogs?" Jeff asked.

"In a way, yes. To tell the truth, when Amelia Carstairs turned fifty she started to get kind of queer. Know what she used to do? She used to come in here and buy vitamin pills to feed her pups." Mr. Jones made a noise between a snort and a chuckle. "Vitamin pills. For dogs!"

Judy was confused. "But I thought you said she gave up breeding."

"She let the kennels go, I mean. But the house was always full of 'em, nearly up to the end. They say she used to raise new litters in the bathrooms. There wasn't much money left, and the place started to go to seed, and she lived there all alone with her dogs and what day help she could get . . ." The druggist's voice trailed off as he saw an adult customer coming in the door. "Afternoon, sir. What can I do for you?"

Jeff sipped his milk shake thoughtfully. "I wonder

why Miss Carstairs moved away," he said half to himself.

Judy's shoulders twitched in a shudder. "Why wouldn't she?" She was remembering the house.

"It was her home," Jeff reminded her. "There was new wallpaper on that little sitting room and the connecting bedroom. You don't wallpaper a place you're planning to leave, do you?"

But Judy was off on another tack, one that looked more promising than any she had navigated all day. "I wonder what she did with her dogs," she mused.

Mr. Jones, coming back just then, answered her question promptly. "Sold 'em," he said. "She finally had to come to it. Over a couple of years, now, she's been letting the last of them go. Had to. Creditors. The butcher and baker and candlestick maker." He chuckled. "The druggist too. Vitamins! Imagine. For dogs!"

"Are you sure she sold *all* her dogs?" Judy questioned.

"Pretty sure," Mr. Jones replied. "She needed money bad." He took Jeff's fifty cents and handed him ten cents change. "Tell you who'd know for sure—he may even have bought one—Mr. Artemus Gross."

"So you see," Judy said, rolling over on her stomach and squinting up at the little old lady who sat very erect in the cypress garden chair, "we're getting nowhere fast."

She and Jeff had just finished telling Mamam the long and involved story of the spaniel mix-up, from the moment Jeff had seen the two black specks bobbing along in the middle of the macadam road to the final remark of Mr. Jones the druggist. Judy had described, with graphic gestures and a little permissible embellishment, her moonlight expedition to Gross Point. Jeff had taken over the story when they approached Carstairs' Castle. And Mamam, through the entire recounting, had crocheted very rapidly, without looking down at her work, her bright eyes darting from one twin to the other as she made small clucking sounds with her teeth.

She was a very satisfactory audience, patient and interested, and in any well-organized mystery the marshaling of the facts should have led all three of them to a clearer view of the case. "Only," as Judy said, "this isn't a neat job. What clues there are go skittering off every which way, without coming back to focus on anything at all."

"Or anybody," added Jeff.

"That doesn't matter," said Mamam briskly. "If they all pointed in one direction there wouldn't be a mystery. You've only scratched the surface of this case. You need to do more probing." She bit the end of her thread with a snapping sound. "Take Ellery Queen. He finds out *everything* before he forms an opinion."

"Ellery Queen?" Judy looked at the erect old lady in astonishment. "I didn't know you read detective stories, Mamam."

"Certainly. Have for years. Never pay more than twenty-five cents for them though. In a case like this now, the technique of some of the famous detectives is very instructive."

"Like Sherlock Holmes?" Jeff suggested, sitting up.

"Sherlock Holmes!" Mamam sounded shocked. "My goodness, boy, he's as out of date as my black bonnet. Queen's your man, or, in certain cases, Sir George Anstruther. Though of course he wouldn't be interested unless there were at least three corpses in the Gross Point woods."

"Corpses!" Judy sat up with a jerk. "Mamam!" She pretended to be horrified.

"Oh, I'm not really serious, child! I'm quite aware that that's more than we can hope for, especially around Wayne." She sighed and shook her head. "The puppies will have to do." Taking up her ball of crochet cotton she jabbed her needle into it firmly, then folded her hands in her lap and glanced from Judy to Jeff. "Now let's get organized."

Judy's jaw dropped an inch, and she looked at her twin. Jeff's mouth was open too, but he was looking at Mamam with a mixture of astonishment and admiration. Neither of them said a word.

"Go get a pencil and paper, Jeffrey," Mamam ordered. She always called the twins by their full Christian names. "We need to get a few things down in black and white."

When he came back she said happily, "Now we'll make a list."

"List?"

"In two columns," Mamam went on. " 'Things We Know' and 'Things We Don't Know.' " She paused a second. "Got it?"

Jeff nodded, half amused but quite willing to humor the old lady, who was one of his favorite persons. It was a pet theory of his that very elderly people and very young people often understood each other exceptionally well. "I've got it," he said.

"Well, what do we know?" Mamam glanced at Judy.

Judy's mind went completely blank. "Not much," she said. "We just suspect."

Mamam shrugged off this unsatisfactory reply. She started counting on her fingers, touching her left thumb with the index finger of her right hand. "One.

The puppies were not going either toward Gross Point or toward Matthews'. We know that."

Jeff wrote it down.

"Two. Lynn recognized them and called them by name at once, before she'd even been home to find they were missing."

"Right," said Jeff.

"Three. The pups were equally friendly with Lynn and with Young Art Gross."

"That confuses things," argued Judy.

"Doesn't matter. It's a fact, isn't it?"

Judy had to nod.

By the time they finished they had quite a sizable list, which filled two sides of a sheet. The items under "Things We Don't Know" were fewer.

"We don't know where the Matthews got the dogs they claim are theirs," Jeff had written. "We don't know whether Miss Carstairs ever sold Mr. Gross any dogs. We don't know where the new puppies up in Lynn's kennel came from. We don't know whether it's a common thing for dogs not to have dewclaws."

"And you don't really know very much about either Lynn or her father," Mamam said briskly. "You don't know how they think and feel, what they're like inside, whether they go to church—or anything. You've got to find out."

"How?" asked Jeff.

"That's your problem. My problem's Young Art Gross. I'll find out whether he's ever had any dealings with Amelia Carstairs. I'm going to call on him to-morrow, for old times' sake. He knows what I thought of his father, but even so, at my age, he can scarcely refuse to let me in."

All that evening Judy and Jeff racked their brains to think of a way to get to know the Matthews better. Finally an idea occurred to Jeff as the direct result of a telephone call from Mr. Davidson. Because of the drought the grass had stopped growing, and Mr. Davidson thought it would do more harm than good to run the lawn mower over it that week.

Jeff was disappointed. He'd been counting on Mr. Davidson's dollar to swell his savings for a new fishing rod. On the other hand, the phone call was a blessing in disguise. It suggested to Jeff the thought that maybe Mr. Matthews could use him as a helper on some of his gardening jobs.

He approached his father with the idea immediately. "D'you think it would be all right to ask?"

"I think so." Mr. Sutherland encouraged a show of initiative in his son. He'd always wanted to get summer jobs when he was a boy, and he understood a yearning for independence in Jeff.

Judy was envious when Jeff told her about his plan. She realized at once that if Mr. Matthews took him on Jeff would be killing two birds with one stone. He'd be making money and at the same time he'd have ample opportunity to learn a good deal about the gardener's present employers.

The next day was Saturday, and Jeff trudged up the hill very early in the morning, in the hope of catching Mr. Matthews before he left for work. Judy trotted along, just for something to do, and stood talking to Lynn by the back door while Jeff interviewed the gardener out by the tumble-down garage.

Already Lynn had the breakfast dishes washed, and through the screen door Judy could see, on a newspaper-covered chair, an open gallon can of white paint.

"I just can't stand this kitchen any longer," Lynn said in explanation. "I'm going to try to paint it myself." She eyed the paint rather dubiously and said the words as though she were attempting an almost impossible task.

"Haven't you ever done any painting?" Judy asked. Lynn shook her head.

"I've done lots," Judy bragged. "I painted my whole room last winter, walls and woodwork and all." Her eyes glistened with interest and she looked from the dun-colored, smoke-stained walls to the inviting paint. "Gosh," she said, "I'd love to help. I haven't got a thing to do all day."

The offer popped out so spontaneously that it never dawned on Judy that it would help her to accomplish the very thing she wanted most to do—to get on more intimate terms with Lynn. Jeff, coming up behind her, heard Lynn say, "But I have only one brush," and Judy reply, "I've got a dandy down home; I'll just run down and get it." He gave his twin credit for a nice piece of strategy, which she didn't deserve at all, and told her that Mr. Matthews would be glad to use him as a helper—as a matter of fact there was a job he could go out on up until about one o'clock this very day.

Jeff left at once with the gardener, rattling off in the old jalopy that had to be hand-cranked. Judy hurried down the hill, to inform the family of Jeff's whereabouts and to collect a pair of overalls and a paintbrush. Mamam, industriously reading the morning *Inquirer* from cover to cover, nodded approvingly. This was going to be a fruitful day.

As a matter of fact, the morning flew for Judy. She loved to paint, because it was work that went fast and showed definite results. Lynn was a little slow and awkward with a brush at first, but she followed Judy's suggestions and learned a few tricks as she went along. By the time a noon whistle blew in the distance a first coat was on three of the walls and the built-in kitchen cabinet.

"Aren't you tired?" asked Lynn. "Wouldn't you like to stop?"

"I'm not tired, but I'm hungry," said Judy bluntly. "If you could give me a sandwich, we could go right on."

The two girls sat on the back steps to eat. There was fresh cow's milk, and Lynn had made cucumber-and-tomato sandwiches with vegetables from her father's truck patch. Judy yawned happily. Everything tasted awfully good.

After lunch Lynn let the pups out of their pen and they gamboled around Judy like frisky colts, spilling over each other's bodies and squealing in delight.

"What do you call them?" Judy asked.

"This one's Boy and that one's Brother." Judy recognized the alliteration that had marked Shadow's and Sambo's names.

"They're really awfully sweet!" Judy laughed, crouching down so they could climb against her and nip at her neck and lick her face.

"Awfully," Lynn admitted, and her eyes suddenly filled with unshed tears. "I can't help loving them. But I *do* wish they were mine!"

Suddenly the pups streaked off, one after the other, to the woods behind the house, where they probably scented a rabbit, and as Judy watched them go she remembered Shadow and Sambo frisking around the lawn down home. Now that she was beginning really to *see* cocker spaniels—to recognize them as individuals, rather than as a breed—she could understand the differences between the two pairs of dogs. These were sweet pups, as she and Lynn agreed, but there had been something about the way Shadow and Sambo moved—about the way they carried their tails and the way their muscles rippled under their silky coats—that put them head and shoulders above Boy and Brother.

Lynn didn't say anything more about the dogs. She

seemed to consider the subject one which it was now fruitless to pursue. She gives up too easily, Judy thought. She ought to have more drive. Yet Lynn's very quality of resignation was the characteristic which made Judy most anxious to help her. Brimming with energy herself, she couldn't bear to see anyone else lethargic and downtrodden, as Lynn appeared to be.

It carried through all the girl's activities. As they finished painting the kitchen Judy's mind was hurrying on to new projects. She was thinking how cunning red-and-white checked cotton curtains would look at the dormer windows, how easy it would be to slap a coat of cold-water paint over the dreadful wallpaper in the living room. Yellow, she'd use—a warm, sunny yellow that would make the whole house seem more cheerful. Definitely, Judy felt, there wasn't enough color in Lynn's life.

"I'd like to study decorating someday," Judy said aloud, as she pulled her paintbrush carefully down the mullion of a window. "I'd like to have a shop of my own, and handle fabrics and combine colors. I know just what I'd call it—'The Little House Shop.' I'd advise people with little houses who didn't have enough money to go to big interior decorators for help."

Lynn looked at Judy in admiration. "That's a nice idea," she said.

"You can do so much with color," Judy went on. "This room is going to look lovely and fresh, all white, but it needs something to make it gay."

"Like what?"

Judy stood back from the window she was painting and cocked her head to one side. "Like bright curtains. Red-and-white checked cotton, and geraniums in the windows. Can't you see them?"

Lynn could, through Judy's eyes, but she would never have thought of them herself. "There's an old checked tablecloth—an enormous one—with a hole in the middle, upstairs. We could cut that up."

Judy realized with gratitude that Lynn had said "we." She was beginning to thaw, to lose some of her proud reserve. "Could we?" Judy cried. "O Lynn, I think they'd be darling. Let's!"

Before the middle of the afternoon they had the curtain-making project settled. Judy was to help, and they'd cut them with short valances, in order to let in plenty of light. Timidly, Judy suggested an even more ambitious idea. She wanted Lynn to let Jeff and herself help to paint the living room. There was a big can of exactly the yellow she had in mind in the garage down home. Mother had bought it for the playroom in the basement, then changed her mind, and Judy was sure she could get it for the asking. The suggestion to Lynn had to be made tactfully though. Lynn would never accept, Judy knew, anything that smacked of charity.

She was delighted and relieved when Lynn agreed, with shy pleasure, that it would be a wonderful idea. She was a little overwhelmed by Judy's generosity, but her enthusiasm was so obviously genuine that Lynn caught some of her zest.

"We could start first thing Monday morning," Judy said. "Jeff can do the ceiling. That's hardest. I think we can do the whole job in a day. Why don't you keep it a secret and surprise your dad?"

They agreed on details as they painted on, and the afternoon hours slipped away, one by one. As they neared the end of the job Judy began to get restless. Jeff would be home by now, and Mamam would be going off to pay her social call on Mr. Artemus Gross. She wanted to get down the hill in time to change her clothes and be ready to greet her on her return. There would be notes to compare, too, with Jeff.

Working rapidly, she finished the last mullion of the casement windows at ten minutes of four. She cleaned her paintbrush and wiped off her hands with a kerosene-soaked rag, promising to return on Monday when she said good-bye to Lynn. Then she raced down the hill, conscious that she herself would have nothing of special interest to report, except that Lynn was just as nice a girl as she'd always considered her to be. She was very hopeful, though, that Jeff and Mamam would come home with more exciting stories. Even before she reached the turn-around by the garage she was calling her brother's name.

"Jeff!"

"Hi."

Jeff, with a pair of shears in his hands, stuck his

head out from behind the high hedge. He was still in his work clothes, and he looked hot and tired, not like a sleuth who has recently made an important discovery. Judy's spirits fell.

"Anything interesting happen?"

"Yep." Jeff's eyes twinkled. "I made two bucks."

Judy stamped her foot. "You know what I mean."

Resuming his hedge-clipping, Jeff turned serious. "Nothing so very interesting. I did find out a few things though. There was another gardener on the place and I had a chance to talk to him a good bit because we were working outside while Mr. Matthews was in the greenhouse."

"Yes?" Judy sounded eager again.

"This guy knows Matthews well. He told me the other places he works. So it'll be easy to check, now, to see whether anybody gave him any dogs. I know for certain these people didn't. They can't bear dogs, this fellow said. Won't have one on the place."

"How'll you check?"

"We can ask, can't we? There's no harm in asking."

"Well . . ." Judy sounded dubious, but she didn't feel like pursuing this question right at the moment. "Is Mamam back yet?"

Jeff shook his head. "She only left a little while ago."

"I'm going up and take a bath then." Judy started off.

"There's just one more thing," Jeff called after her.

"I did something else a little while ago. I called Dr. Clark."

"The vet?" Judy stopped unbuckling her overall straps and turned around.

"Uh-huh."

"Why?"

"I wanted to ask him a couple of questions about dewclaws, just to be sure what Lynn told us was right." He paused and clicked the clipper blades to dislodge a piece of privet caught in the lock.

"Well, was it?" Judy, her faith in Lynn's integrity stronger than ever, sounded defensive.

"Yes," Jeff replied. "Lots of dogs have their dewclaws removed when their tails are cut, just as she said. Some are even born without any."

This added up, in Judy's mind, to exactly zero. As far as she could see neither she nor Jeff could expect any prizes as a result of the day's work. Mamam, she hoped, might do better. Over the noise of the rushing water from the bathroom tap she strained her ears to catch the sound of her returning taxi.

JUDY NEEDN'T HAVE raced through her bath. She was dressed in a flowered-chintz pinafore and down in the swing under the cherry tree before a crunching sound announced the advance of wheels up the drive.

It might, Judy knew, be her mother and dad, who had gone off to look at an antique chest at a dealer's in Paoli. It wouldn't do to get too excited before she was sure. She closed her eyes, planning to count ten, but she didn't play fair. It *was* the taxi! Delighted, she slipped down from the swing and ran around to the front of the house.

The minute Mamam saw her she chuckled and shook her head. "There's nothing to get wrought up about, Judith. Just let me take off my bonnet, now. I'll tell you all about it soon enough."

Jeff joined them on the terrace in a few minutes, as anxious as his twin to hear the story of the call at Gross Point, but less willing to display his impatience.

Mamam eased herself cautiously into a low garden chair, which she considered the invention of a weak-minded moron, and began.

"Young Art wasn't home when I got there," she said, "but I made up my mind I'd wait a bit. I let the taxi fellow go and told him to come back in an hour. After a while Young Art came in."

Judy wondered whether Mamam had been shown into the library which she herself knew so well, but she hesitated to interrupt her.

"Young Art had a dog with him—not a black one, a copper-colored one he said he'd had down to the veterinarian's. I can tell you this: that boy was plenty surprised to see me." Mamam wagged her head. "But he knew me right off!" she continued with pride. "He said, 'Well, well, this *is* a surprise, Miss Jennie!' and I said right back, 'I see you have your father's faculty for remembering names.'"

Judy wriggled impatiently. If Mamam had a story to tell, she wished she'd get on with it.

But the old lady wasn't to be hurried. She told the tale in her own way, about how they sat down and chatted, Mr. Gross obviously perplexed that he should receive a call from his father's old neighbor, especially since he remembered vaguely that they had been on lukewarm terms. He was cordial enough, though, even offered Mamam tea.

"Did you talk about dogs?" Judy broke in.

"Not much," Mamam said, to the twins' astonishment. "There's been a lot of talk already about dogs. I couldn't see there was much more to say. We talked about Miss Amelia Carstairs."

"Miss Carstairs!" Judy and Jeff spoke the name together, and Judy added, "Does Mr. Gross know her?"

"That's what I wanted to find out," Mamam explained.

"And did you?" Judy burst forth.

Mamam raised her hand in a peremptory gesture. "Sh, child! Let me go my own gait." She settled back ever so slightly in her chair and put the five fingers of one hand against the five fingers of the other. "I've noticed that when Colonel Primrose has something on his mind he wants to find out, he often talks around the subject, instead of striking right at it. That's not my way, normally. But in a case like this . . ." Mamam's thin voice trailed off.

Judy's chest was tight with impatience. Colonel Primrose, she knew, must be one of Mamam's detective-story heroes. All she could hope was that he wouldn't lead his devotee too far afield.

Luck was with her. Mamam's mind snapped back to Gross Point and she began to reconstruct the conversation for the twins.

"I mentioned to Young Art," she said, "that since I was visiting in the neighborhood I planned to make some other calls. I told him I especially wanted to go over to see poor Amelia Carstairs."

"I didn't know . . ." Judy blurted out.

"Neither did Young Art," Mamam replied happily, without waiting for her to finish. "He couldn't have the slightest idea that I wouldn't know Miss Carstairs from a hole in the ground. He bit just like a salmon at a fly. 'Carstairs' place is closed up,' he said right off. 'Miss Amelia has moved out West.' "

Mamam chuckled reminiscently. "I said: 'Fancy that now! I thought she loved the old place. I'm surprised she'd leave it.' Young Art just shrugged. He said: 'Maybe she had to. It was heavily mortgaged, you know.' "

" ' 'Course I didn't know,' I snapped back. 'I keep my nose out of other people's business.' "

At this point Judy bit her lower lip with her small white teeth and looked shocked, but Mamam waved her hand airily.

Mr. Gross had apparently made up his mind to humor the old lady. He let this remark pass and suggested that she might like to see around his house. Mamam described the tour of inspection. "Quite a place he has there," she admitted. "Mighty different from the row house on Second Street where his pop started out. I wouldn't like to swear to how he got the money that bought it, but that's neither here nor there."

She went on with her story. "I didn't care much for the living room or library. Heavy, foreign stuff. But the dining room quite took my eye. There were a dozen rose-carved Victorian chairs as nice as any I've ever seen. When I went up and patted one Young Art sort of smiled. 'They came from an estate near here,' he said."

Judy remembered at once that there had been no chairs in the dining room at Carstairs' Castle. She said as much to Mamam, and the old lady grinned back and nodded her head. "I'm not surprised," she said. " 'Course those chairs could have been bought out of any one of a dozen old homes. We don't know anything for certain. Still and all, I wouldn't be surprised if Young Art knew Miss Amelia Carstairs a good deal better than he's letting on."

Judy considered this possibility. If Mr. Gross knew Miss Carstairs well, it stood to reason he'd have been in an excellent position to buy one or more of her dogs, as the druggist had suggested he might. She supposed this had also occurred to Mamam, or why would she have cannily pursued this tack?

"Did you ask Mr. Gross," she couldn't resist inquiring, "if he'd bought any of Miss Carstairs' dogs?"

"No, I didn't," Mamam replied, "and for the same reason I didn't tell him I was staying down here with you. I couldn't see any point to letting Young Art know I was interested in dogs at all. I figured there was no sense putting him on his guard if he had anything to hide."

Jeff smiled, thinking that Mamam was pretty shrewd. "Did he show you his kennels?"

To Judy's disappointment, Mamam shook her head.

"I could see the kennel house, though, through the dining-room windows. So I walked over and said, 'What's that?' Young Art told me then that he was interested in breeding cocker spaniels, and I pretended I wasn't impressed a bit. 'Hmph,' I said, 'Crazy Joe Collins, that used to live back of your old place in Camden, was a breeder of dogs. Used to sell 'em too, ten or fifteen dollars apiece. But it sounds to me like a pretty peculiar hobby for a rich man.'

"Well," Mamam went on, "that got Young Art's dander up, just as I thought it would. He explained, very supercilious-like, that there was a great deal of difference between ordinary dog-breeding and the breeding of show dogs such as he's interested in. The Grosses were always ones to brag, and he said, as though I was just a know-nothing old lady, 'Why, do you know what a couple of pups I'm raising right now are worth?'

"I said, 'No. What?'

"He said, 'A thousand dollars apiece.'

"I said, 'Hmph! I'd like to see them!' and he came right back with, 'I'll have them brought in.' "

Judy clapped her hands. "O Mamam," she cried, "did you see them? Did you really see Shadow and Sambo?"

Jeff was leaping to more practical hopes. "You didn't get a chance to find out about the dewclaws—"

"No, I didn't," Mamam said sorrowfully. "Young Art had the pups brought in, right enough, but the kennelman paraded them past me on leads. They're cute rascals, with their long ears and sad eyes."

"They're *darlings!*" sighed Judy.

"But they didn't look like any thousand dollars to me."

Jeff looked at Mamam. "Did you say so?"

"'Course not," Mamam replied emphatically. "I just said, 'Any Carstairs strain in these dogs?'"

Both Judy and Jeff gasped. It was a question they never would have thought of, let alone venture.

"I just wanted to see the look on Young Art's face," Mamam went on. "It wasn't that I expected to get an affirmative answer."

"How did he look?" Jeff asked.

Mamam hesitated. "He looked—well, almost as if somebody'd quick drawn a curtain down over his eyes. I guess he never liked Miss Carstairs. He said, 'You'll see these pups go farther than any Carstairs dog ever went!'"

"If I live," Mamam had retorted very piously, and shortly afterward Mr. Gross had ushered her out. As she climbed into the taxi with the aid of her cane and the driver's arm Young Art had turned suddenly curious. Mamam chuckled when she remembered the way he had stuck his head in at the open window.

"By the way," he had said, "where did you say you were visiting?"

"I didn't say," Mamam had retorted, "but it's at the Sutherlands', if you'd like to know."

Judy considered this admission to have been a tactical blunder, but Mamam said: "Not a bit. He could find out, quick enough, if he wanted to ask."

"Did he seem surprised?" asked Jeff.

"He seemed mad," Mamam said with an impish smile. "He got quite red in the face."

Although Mamam apparently considered the visit quite productive, Judy couldn't see that it helped one jot to find some path which would lead them out of the tangled maze of possibility and supposition into which they had wandered. With her head in her hands she sat and daydreamed, while Jeff answered questions as to how he had spent his day. When it came her turn to report, Judy told Mamam frankly that she hadn't discovered a thing. She'd had fun painting the kitchen, and she was glad they'd agreed on the living room project, but as far as learning anything that might help in solving the spaniel mystery, she simply hadn't.

"All I know," she added, "is that I'm more convinced than ever that Lynn's a perfectly sincere and honest girl."

"That's a lot," said Mamam brightly. "We'll see what we will see."

There was little to be seen over the rest of the week end. Sunday developed into another scorching day, and after church the entire Sutherland family relaxed in the shade of the pine tree near the terrace, reading the Sunday papers and chatting idly, trying to keep their minds off the heat. Only one event, of minor importance, disturbed the peace and quiet of the afternoon. Boy and Brother, tongues lolling, came bounding down the hill from the Matthews' to cavort around the Sutherlands' lawn like two boys playing hooky. On their heels came Lynn.

"They haven't much sense," she apologized. "The minute the pen door is open they think it's a signal that they can run away."

The twins introduced Lynn to Mamam, who held the girl's hand for a minute and looked inquiringly into her gray eyes. "She's nice," Mamam announced after Lynn had left. That was all she said.

Judy took the opportunity to ask her father whether she might give Lynn the remains of the gallon of cold-water paint which she had in mind for the Matthews' living room.

"Of course," George Sutherland agreed at once. "Glad to have it used." Then the telephone rang, and he went into the house to answer it while Judy outlined to her mother the plans she and Lynn had for doing over the walls of the little house on the hill.

Sheila Sutherland was interested. She loved color and warmth in a house herself, and she had a feeling for polished old wood that she hoped her daughter would inherit. Judy asked her advice about what could be done with the dreadful mission furniture, if Lynn should wish to go farther after the walls were finished, and the two talked about decorating for ten or fifteen minutes.

"We're going to start tomorrow morning," Judy said with anticipation just as her father came out of the house again. "I promised Lynn."

George Sutherland heard this remark and he shook his head in mock sadness. "Now that's too bad, Judy," he said. "A client of mine just called and I've got to drive up to Blue Lake. I was thinking of asking you and Jeff to ride along so that you could have a swim."

Jeff, who had been sprawled on the ground with the funnies, sat up at once. "Boy!" he said. "Will that be keen!"

Judy's expression mixed anticipation with a mild concern. She looked at her mother. "D'you suppose Lynn would mind if we put it off?"

Mrs. Sutherland smiled back at Judy. "I shouldn't think so. Why don't you walk up the hill after dinner and explain?"

Jeff sauntered up the hill at Judy's side. It had been a dull day, humid and uninteresting. Mr. Matthews was weeding his truck patch and it made Jeff think of the old saw about the busman's holiday. Lynn was sitting idly on the worn front steps.

When Judy explained why she wanted to put off the paint job until Tuesday Lynn said at once: "That's quite all right. Of course I understand!" but the twins both saw a shadow of disappointment settle over her eyes and she glanced instinctively toward her dad.

"It isn't all right, really," Judy replied at once. "You wanted to do it tomorrow especially. Why?"

Lynn tried to shrug off the question, but Judy pinned her down. "It doesn't matter much at all," she finally said. "It's just that Daddy's birthday happens to be Tuesday and I thought it would be fun to surprise him. He's going to be out tomorrow night anyway. Please don't worry, Judy. Tuesday will be just as good."

But Judy knew how Lynn felt. She understood feelings far better than ideas and she could picture Lynn getting up on Tuesday morning and leading her father into the freshly painted living room as a birthday surprise. It just wouldn't be so good to do it Tuesday night. She stood for a minute, thinking. Then her eyes brightened. "Look," she said, "how would this be? Jeff and I should be home from the lake by four o'clock. Suppose we were to have an early supper and come up and work on the room tomorrow night? Cold-water paint goes like lightning, you know. With Jeff and you and me all working, we could do the whole room in a few hours."

"It would be cooler then too," Jeff put in. "I think that's a swell idea."

They had some trouble convincing Lynn that this was a sensible plan, but finally the twins won the argument and left with the promise to return about six o'clock the next evening.

"We'll be finished long before ten-thirty," Judy insisted, naming the hour Lynn expected her father home.

"We'd better be!" Jeff added. "Except over week ends, mother keeps us on a ten o'clock curfew."

Monday dawned clear and as hot as ever. For Judy and Jeff, the hours at the lake passed so rapidly that they couldn't believe it was time to start home when their father came down from the hotel for them. Judy dozed most of the way to Wayne, while Jeff chatted with his dad.

"Ever hear of a man by the name of Fitzhugh in the dog business?" he asked when he got a chance.

Mr. Sutherland considered. "Yes," he said, "there's a judge. Let me see—I remember seeing his name in the paper just the other day. R. J. Fitzhugh, that's it. Judges cockers and springers at the big shows. Why?" He looked at Jeff closely, hoping the boy still wasn't interested in the puppy mix-up, which the lawyer had long since considered closed.

Jeff shrugged. "He's a friend of Mr. Gross's. It's an odd name. I just wondered, that's all."

"He's a pretty important man in his line," Mr. Sutherland said. "I suppose Art Gross would cultivate the big shots."

When they reached home, lulled and lazy from the motion of the car, both the twins were beginning to regret their insistence on going through with the painting job this evening. Supper only partially revived them, and they changed into overalls and trudged up the hill gloomily, trying to stifle yawns.

Lynn, by contrast, was fresh and full of anticipation. Everything was in readiness for the painting. The living room woodwork was scrubbed, the furniture pushed away from the walls, and the floor covered with newspaper. Once the tedious job of mixing paint was finished, they divided it into three different containers. While Jeff mounted a stepladder and started on the ceiling Judy and Lynn each attacked a wall.

Gradually the twins revived. With all three of them working at once, the job, as Judy had prophesied, did indeed go fast. The paint went on rather dark, but it dried to a pale, cool yellow which erased all trace of brush strokes. Outside, the sun slipped slowly down behind the hill and the long summer twilight faded to darkness. Judy stood back and surveyed her work. "There," she said, "that leaves us only one more wall to do. You start at that end, Lynn, and I'll start at this. We'll meet at the windows."

"You'll meet," Jeff added, "directly under my stepladder, and if you're not doggone careful, Judy, you'll come out of this deal a blonde."

"That's something I've always wanted to be," Judy replied, looking at Lynn's fair hair, which was twisted in a casual knot on top of her head for the sake of coolness. The ghost of a breeze was lifting a strand which fell forward on her forehead and for the first time in days Judy thought she sniffed cooler air. At the same moment thunder began to rumble in the distance. "Maybe it's going to rain!" both she and Lynn said at once.

"Philopena!" Jeff teased.

But Judy wasn't paying any attention. Paintbrush in hand, she had stopped working for a minute and was standing in front of the open windows, peering out into the darkness. She wasn't just looking for rain, Jeff realized as he noticed the angle of her head. She seemed to be listening for something.

The sharp crack of thunder, much closer now, interrupted his thought, and at the same moment Judy turned and went back to the patch of dingy wallpaper she was painting.

"If we have to close the windows we'll smother," said Lynn conversationally.

"If we don't," Jeff replied with equal nonchalance, "we'll probably drown."

Lightning streaked for an instant across the sky outside, and the porch and lawn blazed white. It exploded in another clap of thunder, which rumbled furiously for a moment, then retreated to nag grouchily from the woods behind the house.

"Hey, we're going to catch it fast!" Jeff gave a last swipe of his paintbrush to the ceiling and picked up his can of paint. Outside, in the pen, the dogs started to bark in shrill excitement. Judy, without speaking, walked back to the front windows and stood again, peering out.

"I'd better get the pups," Lynn started to say, but she hadn't finished speaking before another thunderclap broke deafeningly over their heads, drowning both her voice and the barking of the dogs.

Jeff was slipping down the ladder. "I'll close these windows. What about the ones upstairs?"

Lynn, who had already started for the door, turned. "I forgot. They're open too!"

"You get those; I'll get the dogs!" Judy streaked past Lynn to the porch, down the steps, and around to the side of the house. Lynn dashed upstairs and Jeff started slamming down the living room windows with quick abandon.

The first big, spatting raindrops hit the roof with the next concussion of thunder. Lynn clattered downstairs as the deluge started and Jeff hurried after her to meet Judy.

"She'll be drenched!" Lynn shouted.

"What in the heck's she doing?" Jeff shouted back. "She's had plenty of time—" In the glare of a taut

ribbon of lightning his eyes caught a glimpse of a vacant expanse of grass. The pen was at the side of the house, out of sight. "Judy!" Together he and Lynn raced down the porch steps into the rain. They both seemed to sense something at once—something indefinably wrong.

"Judy!"

Without the aid of the lightning the world was a dark torrent. Lynn and Jeff both tried to pierce the din of the next thunderclap with their ears as they rounded the corner of the house. Lightning flashed again, illuminating the pen. The door was open. The dogs were gone. And Judy was nowhere in sight!

13 "HEY! JUDY!" JEFF CALLED, HIS
changing voice breaking on his twin's name.
"Judy! Where are you? Let the dogs go!" Lynn
put her hands to her mouth to make a trumpet as
she shouted.

But no reply reached the pair through the wind and rain. Together they ran around toward the back steps. Confound those pups, anyway! Jeff was thinking. They never did have Shadow's and Sambo's quiet aggressiveness; they were nervous and skittish, probably frightened to death by the storm.

Lynn was thinking the same thing. "When she opened the pen door they probably bolted. They haven't an ounce of sense!" she told Jeff breathlessly, shaking the rain from her face. This was a fine way to climax the evening—everybody getting thoroughly wet!

Neither the pups nor Judy were at the back of the house, so Lynn and Jeff continued their dash around to the front again. A flash of lightning lighted the road down the hill for an instant, and though it ran rivers of water in its deep ruts it was quite empty. Gasping, Lynn beat Jeff to the comparative shelter of the front porch.

"Judy!" By now she must have either captured the

dogs or given up the chase. Lynn and Jeff, half-laughing, slid across the wet floor boards to the door. But the living room, its fresh paint glaring under the overhead electric light, was empty and quiet. No paw marks stained the newspaper-covered floor. No wet soles left their imprint. The silence of the house under the canopy of the noisy storm seemed suddenly oppressive. The thunder, when it came again, carried a threat of danger. Lynn looked anxiously at Jeff and Jeff stared back at Lynn, baffled. To hide his mounting concern he made his tone sound annoyed. "Where can that kid have gone?"

Lynn spread her hands helplessly. "I—I can't imagine!" Her smooth forehead, glistening with rain, puckered into worried knots.

Jeff, just because he felt the need of action, half opened the door and called again, though he was certain his sister wasn't in the house. Everything in the vacant room etched itself sharply on his brain—the three paint cans, the unfinished fourth wall, the huddled furniture, the rickety stepladder, the clock leaning against the second step of the stairs, with its hands at 9:25. The last time he'd noticed the clock it had been 9:15, and he'd thought they were going to finish the paint job sooner than they'd expected. Now the painting seemed of minor importance. He didn't really care if it was never finished. He only wanted to get Judy back to the house. Little fool! Chasing off after those dogs! Didn't she realize that in a bad electrical storm like this trees could crash, people could be struck?

"I'm going to go back toward the woods," he said. "I couldn't be any wetter."

"I'll come too." Lynn's voice was small with worry. The dogs, while she claimed no ownership—indeed, she considered them interlopers—were nevertheless her responsibility for the time being. If anything should happen to Judy because of them she'd never be able to forgive herself. Following closely on Jeff's heels, she ran across the ragged patch of grass.

The woods which rose just behind the Matthews' clearing stretched in a moonlike curve for a scant half mile to the highway, running west, and for perhaps twice that distance to the east. They were only a few hundred yards deep and they ended in the plowed land of a farm which faced on another road. Jeff knew them only slightly, but Lynn knew them well. They were laced with bridle paths, and it was toward one of these that she headed, feeling that for either the pups or for Judy it would have been the most obvious route.

Jeff paused to skirt the truck patch, but Lynn ran right across it, ignoring possible damage to the rows of vegetables, so that she reached the edge of the clearing ahead of the boy. The storm, far from abating, seemed to be getting more violent with every fresh burst of thunder. As she waited for Jeff to catch up, fear clutched at Lynn's throat. The woods was certainly no place to be on a night like this!

Yet what could they do? Judy, to have disappeared so suddenly, could never have taken the road down the hill. In that one bright flash of light they had made sure of that. Only the shelter of the woods could have hidden her so quickly from their eyes. Anxious to catch the pair of terrified pups, impetuous, and careless of any danger to herself, it was entirely possible that Judy might have run after them down the first lane that opened between the trees.

The bridle path immediately ahead was the clearest course. As Jeff caught up, Lynn told him so in a few hurried words. Then, taking a long breath, she plunged after the boy, in among the black trunks which rose menacing and unfamiliar.

When the trees closed over their heads, Jeff and Lynn had to slow down to a sloshing walk. Roots curved above the spongy leaf mold, ready to trip the unwary. The path wound in and out like a lizard, slippery and black. Rain pelted through the heavy branches, dripped in rivulets from the leaves. Intermittent flashes of white light outlined writhing arms which locked above the full-skirted dogwoods, and with every vehement thunderbolt Lynn cringed.

Jeff, fumbling in the blind darkness that followed one flash, got off the path and smacked, with a breathtaking bump, into the trunk of an oak. "Darn!" he gasped when he recovered. "I can't see a thing!"

"I'll go ahead," Lynn said. "I know the road." It cost her an effort to make the offer. She was badly frightened. She shuddered at the noise of thunder when she was safely in the house, and out here in the woods it seemed doubly awful, full of madness and destruction. Besides, her reason told her it would have been insane of Judy to come so far.

"Let me!" Jeff protested, realizing that Lynn was scared, yet at the same time feeling that her suggestion might speed their progress. As he spoke he felt the girl push past him and he could do nothing but fall in behind her.

"Judy!"

"Hy-ah! Judy!"

The boy's voice and the girl's went on, calling the name. Judy would have to be very close if she were to hear them. Both Lynn and Jeff felt their own words flung back into their throats by the driving wind.

Overhead, the branches of trees whipped like the blades of a giant electric fan. The thunder seemed even more shattering than before. It was bursting directly above the searchers now, in a deafening blitz of sound. Drenched and hoarse, they kept on calling: "Judy!"

It began to seem ridiculous to Jeff to go on. Yet to turn back seemed cowardly. If Judy had really followed the pups up to these woods, it was their job to find her. A wet twig snapped back against his cheek with a sting, and Lynn called over her shoulder, "We ought to be almost through."

Jeff strained ahead, almost beside the girl now. The next flash of lightning showed a break in the trees and below them stretched a broad field of young corn, bent almost to the ground by the wind and pelting rain.

They stood with their shoulders touching and looked out across the sloping field, to where a house in the distance showed a small light. When the darkness turned momentarily to day they strained their eyes to see a figure, a hint of unexpected movement in the corn, but they could have been utterly alone in the world, so vacant it seemed. Jeff called his twin's name again and again, but not even an echo came back to mock him. Drearily he turned to Lynn. "We may as well go home."

"Closer to the highway," Lynn said, "there's another path that cuts back to our place. We may as well try that." She dreaded the thought of re-entering the woods. Anything to put it off for another few minutes!

Discouraged, Jeff wanted to say, "Oh, let's go home the way we came," but it didn't seem really fair to Judy. "All right," he agreed.

Together they walked over the soggy hummocks of the plowed field along the edge of the woods. Every few seconds they paused to shout, hands cupped to their mouths, but the trees rose like a wall against their feeble voices.

"Here it is," Lynn said finally, and though Jeff could see no path he turned mechanically back toward the woods.

If to stumble through that dense grove for the first time had been terrifying, for Lynn it was three times as bad to start back. Earlier, she had been spurred by hope and a kind of crazy excitement, but now nothing relieved her fear and anxiety. Her face and hands

were scratched by straggling branches. The shoulder
of her shirt was torn and she was soaked to the skin.
Brambles caught at her wet hair and twisted it painfully. Her shoes were so heavy with water that her feet
dragged. Only the fact that Jeff was right behind her
gave her any comfort at all. She shuddered, thinking
what it would be like for Judy to be lost somewhere
in these woods—alone.

Jeff pushed along without a word. He felt that he
was living in a bad nightmare—that he'd wake up,
surely, and find that Judy had been right there all the
time. Even the thunder of the storm ceased to seem
real. He no longer flinched at the pulsating bombs of
sound that rocked the earth. He followed Lynn blind-
ly, bent almost double to clear the low-hanging
branches of the smaller trees. Twice he wandered off
the path and once Lynn missed a turn and found herself brought up short by a tight thicket of thorny
bushes.

Finally they stopped calling, except for sporadic at-
tempts to make their hoarse voices pierce the blackness
and the pounding rain. It began to seem impossible
to them that Judy should be out alone in this. Surely
they'd find her safe at home when they got there!
Surely they'd been overzealous and foolish to believe—

"Ee-e-e!" Lynn's unconscious cry spelled pure terror. She fell back against Jeff and clutched him, her
hands biting like claws into his arm.

"What's the matter?"

"There!" In the darkness Jeff couldn't see Lynn's shaking finger point. "In the path!" she almost sobbed. "I touched something. There!"

Now, when they needed its help, the lightning was unkind. The blackness was like velvet, smothering them, and under its shroud, what?

It took almost more courage than Jeff possessed to loosen Lynn's clinging hands and move forward, but he kept saying to himself: "I'm a man. I've got to." His left foot hit a stone. He stumbled slightly. Then, recovering himself, he came up against something heavy and soft. . . .

The lightning flashed, giving them an instant's release from darkness, and in that split second Jeff and Lynn whispered at once, "Judy!"

Jeff was down on his knees in the path, feeling for his sister's shoulders, turning her, gently. "She must be hurt . . ."

"She could have stumbled," Lynn, beside him, tried to help. "In the dark she could have stumbled . . ."

"She's sure out cold." Jeff didn't know why, but finding Judy made everything seem suddenly normal again. He wasn't especially frightened now. He didn't anticipate the worst. He felt curiously optimistic and relieved.

Feeling the rain on her face, now upturned, Judy stirred and moaned.

"Judy!" Jeff shook her gently. "Judy!"

"We must be close to home. We could carry her," Lynn said.

Jeff hitched his arm more firmly under Judy's shoulders. "Maybe we'd better."

It wasn't easy, but somehow they supported her limp body between them, pushing aside the branches with their shoulders and backs. They struggled forward a few yards, rested, then went on again. It was a matter of five minutes before they reached the clearing behind the Matthews' house.

The storm was slackening now. The thunder was worrying the countryside over the next ridge of hills. But the light in the living room furnished a beacon, and Judy was stirring, trying to help herself. "Let me walk. I'm all right now," she sighed.

Jeff and Lynn blinked as they pushed open the door and half carried, half pulled Judy to the nearest chair. The electric light, unshaded and glaring, blinded them momentarily, but Judy didn't fight against it. She kept her eyes fast shut and turned a little, letting her cheek rest against the back of the chair.

Lynn knelt down and started to rub Judy's hands briskly. "Can you talk, Judy? Can you tell us if you're hurt?"

For what seemed an endless minute Judy didn't say anything, then, as though in slow motion, her left hand moved toward her forehead. "My head aches," she said in a whisper.

Lying, as she had been when they found her, face down in the path, her wet hair was plastered with leaves and twigs and her face was wet and dirty. Lynn got quietly to her feet and went to the kitchen for a clean dish towel, which she dampened and brought back to use in cleaning Judy's face. She found Jeff touching his twin's hair, right above her forehead, with gentle, exploring fingers.

"She has a beaut of a bump!" he said.

Lynn felt it too, and whistled softly. "I'll say!" Then she wiped Judy's face with the wet cloth tenderly, smoothing back from her forehead the clinging wet tendrils of hair.

"Thanks a lot." Judy still felt disinclined to open her eyes, but she felt an effort was expected of her. "I'll be all right now, really," she murmured. "What did I do? Pass out?"

"You sure did!" her brother said.

Lynn flung the cloth over the stair rail and started to clear the couch of its newspaper covering. "Bring her over here, Jeff. She ought to lie down."

"I'll get it all wet," Judy protested feebly.

"That doesn't matter. It'll dry." Lynn took off Judy's wet shoes and socks and rubbed her wet feet. Inside the house, which had been shut up, it was warm, but outside the storm had dropped the temperature sharply. The girl was thoroughly chilled.

Jeff stood by feeling helpless, but Lynn bustled around, running upstairs for her bathrobe and a couple of aspirin tablets, making Judy slip out of her wet overalls and into the light robe. Finally, to Jeff's relief, his twin managed a smile. Her voice sounded almost normal when she scolded Lynn: "Now relax. *Honestly* I'm all right! Did you get the puppies? That's what I want to know."

"The puppies?" Simultaneously Lynn and Jeff realized that they hadn't given the pups a single thought in the harrowing half hour just past. It seemed incredible to Jeff, when he looked at the clock still leaning crazily against the stair tread, that it had been such a short time ago that he and Lynn had left the house to search the strip of woods. Both the girl and the boy looked at Judy stupidly. "N—no," stammered Jeff, "we didn't."

Judy touched the bump on her head ruefully. "You mean I got this for nothing?"

"Don't worry," Lynn said soothingly. "They'll turn up. You just rest for a while until your head stops hurting and try not to think. You gave us a bad scare. We weren't worrying about the dogs."

"But—" Judy started, then gave up and closed her eyes again. At the same moment Jeff and Lynn heard the chug of a tired motor as it pulled a car up the rocky drive.

"Daddy!" Lynn took one look at the incredible disorder of the room. Here a patch of unpainted wall or ceiling. There a dripping paint can or a brush flung hastily down. On the floor sodden layers of newspaper which had soaked up pools of water from around her feet or Jeff's. Judy, inert on the couch. Jeff's face bleeding from a dozen scratches. And herself? She hadn't thought for a second of how she must appear. Suddenly she burst into laughter. "A fine birthday present this is!"

Her remark, though softly spoken and meant for Jeff, aroused Judy. "O Lynn! This is dreadful! What will your father think?"

Lynn couldn't stop giggling. "He'll think a cyclone has struck us."

"Which," added Jeff, "will be just about right."

Mr. Matthews indeed looked astonished when he put his head in at the living room door. A mild-mannered, slight man, he had always reminded Judy slightly of Eddie Cantor. "He looks like a victim of circumstance," she'd said once to Jeff, but Jeff had just snorted. "You make things up," he had replied.

Now Mr. Matthews just stood in the doorway, his eyes very wide open, and his lips formed a single word: "Well!"

Lynn went over to him, still smiling. "I'm sorry, Daddy! This—this was to have been a birthday surprise, but it got sidetracked."

Mr. Matthews looked around in mild dismay, and Jeff, unexpectedly recovering his own sense of humor, cried, "I'll say it did!"

Judy managed to get to an upright position on the couch and smile weakly, but she let Jeff and Lynn do the explaining. "It'll look lovely, Daddy, when it's finished. Really it will," Lynn said, her eyes sweeping the blotched, half-dry walls.

Mr. Matthews lacked imagination, but Judy decided he was a really good sport. He made an honest effort to keep his voice from sounding dubious when he said, "I don't doubt it."

Judy's mouth quirked at the corners. "Wait till to-morrow!" she promised encouragingly.

Mr. Matthews' eyes swept the dark girl wrapped in his daughter's bathrobe for the first time. "What's the matter with you, young lady?" Then he glanced at Jeff and his daughter. "You're all soaking wet!"

Jeff took up the tale. "The storm started suddenly. Lynn and I were closing windows, so Judy ran out to get the dogs. They must have been terrified. Instead of following her in they ran away."

"Only—" Judy started, then stopped as Jeff's voice continued: "Judy ran after them. Up to the woods. Lynn and I couldn't find her. She must have tripped on a root. Was that it, Judy?"

"I—I guess so. I just remember pitching forward and hitting my head. Between lightning flashes it was so awfully dark!"

"We looked for half an hour," Jeff went on. "We never have found the dogs."

"They'll turn up," Lynn said, trying to be comforting.

Mr. Matthews nodded his head. "Sure. I've seen a

few other spaniels like that—nervous and unpredict-
able. Once when I was taking a dog up to a boarding
kennel the fool pooch got scared and bolted. Hid out
in the woods for days before he got so hungry he had
to come in for food."

Judy murmured, "I'm awfully sorry—" but Mr.
Matthews stopped her.

"Don't you worry a bit," he said. "I'm just feelin'
mighty bad you had such a time of it. Shadow and
Sambo might've been worth a crack on the head, but
not those two loony pups."

To Judy a puppy was a puppy, something to be
sheltered and loved. She wanted to protest that she'd
do the same thing again for any dog, but she was afraid
Mr. Matthews wouldn't understand. Furthermore, she
was getting very sleepy and her head, in spite of the
aspirin, still ached. When the gardener offered to take
Jeff and her down the hill in his car she agreed meekly.
She really would like to get to bed!

The twins went in through the kitchen and up the
back stairs to their rooms. Mamam, they knew, would
already be asleep, and they could hear the voices of
their mother and dad as they chatted with bridge
guests across the card table. Judy hung up Lynn's
robe, drew water for a bath, and draped the rest of her
wet clothes over the window seat. In ten minutes she
was in bed, her head throbbing less now that it was on
a soft pillow. She could hear Jeff still banging around
in the bathroom and she called to him drowsily.

"Jeff!"

Jeff, in striped pajama pants, opened the door to her bedroom. "Huh?"

Judy raised herself cautiously on one elbow. "You know, Jeff," she said, "it's a funny thing. The pen door was open and the dogs were gone before I ever got out there. D'you suppose the lightning could've done that?"

14 THE MINUTE JUDY OPENED HER eyes the next morning she sneezed. Sleepily she rubbed her nose. Then she sneezed again. Wriggling down under the sheet and summer blanket she closed her eyes once more and swallowed experimentally. There was no doubt about it. Her throat was sore.

"You stay in bed," Mrs. Sutherland commanded when she felt her daughter's forehead a few minutes later. "Summer colds aren't to be trifled with."

"But, Mother!"

"No but's."

Judy lay and fumed. There was so much to be done! There was the painting of Lynn's living room to finish, and Judy had especially wanted to be in at the end of the job, so that she could make some suggestions for rearranging furniture. There was the swimming pool to be inspected hopefully. Perhaps the storm would have swelled the brook that fed it. There were the pups to be found, if they hadn't already returned, bedraggled and contrite, to their pen. It was rather pleasant, sometimes, to while away a dreary winter school day in bed with a cold in the head, but on a summer day bed was a prison. Particularly was it absurd to be confined to the house on a day that dawned as fresh and sparkling and blissfully cool as this!

Judy could hear Jeff, outside, whistling. Why didn't he, she fretted, run up the hill and see if the pups had come home? She could hear Mamam's cane, tapping on the uncarpeted stairs, then retiring toward the dining room. That Mamam would spend the better part of the day with her Judy was sure. The anticipation of telling her about last night's adventure was at least something to look forward to.

As she lay staring out the casement window at the bright blue sky the timing bell on the electric stove rang. Judy began to think about food. That bell meant the soft-boiled eggs would be ready for the family breakfast. Sometime soon a tray would be coming upstairs for her. If Jeff brought the tray, she'd make sure he hustled up to the Matthews' first thing. Maybe she could *will* that Jeff would bring it. If she concentrated very hard and said, over and over, "Jeff, *you* bring the tray," maybe he wouldn't be able to help himself. It was worth a try.

Judy blew her nose and turned on her side, leaning on one elbow. It seemed a better position for concentrating. "Jeff, you bring the tray," she began, thinking the words energetically. Her head felt heavy and stuffy and she seemed constantly on the verge of another sneeze. "Jeff, you bring the tray." She used to play this game when she was a little girl. Sometimes it worked, sometimes it didn't. But it was fun, anyway. "Jeff, you bring the tray." She caught sight of her reflection in the dressing-table mirror. Her eyes looked puffy and unattractive. "Jeepers," she complained aloud to her own image, "this would happen to me!"

This broke into her train of thought, and she blamed herself for the fact that eventually it was not Jeff, but her mother, who carried the tray upstairs.

"Thanks, Mommy," she said automatically. "Is Jeff around?"

"He's gone to Wayne, dear, on an errand for me. He'll be back in an hour."

An hour! It might as well have been a week. The orange juice and cereal and egg were tasteless in Judy's mouth. Her lower lip pushed forward.

"Did you want him especially? Is there anything I can do?"

Judy shook her head. "D'you think," she asked, trying to sound very bright and healthy, "that I could get up by noon?"

Mrs. Sutherland, who had been regaled by her son with the account of Judy's mishap in the storm, shook her head. "You'd better count on staying in bed all day, Judy. There's no use courting trouble."

Grimly, Judy settled down. She gargled obediently and, coming back from the bathroom, selected two mysteries which she had read only once from the low shelves under the window seat. Climbing back in bed, she stacked one pillow on top of the other, wriggled until her shoulders were comfortable against them, and tried to distract her mind from the serious questions of the black spaniel case with the adventures of a heroine who was impervious alike to summer colds and to the necessity for running errands.

The story concerned the discovery and return to his throne of the kidnaped young prince of Sylvania. The heroine did a masterful job of it, braving perils that would have made Judy collapse in a heap, aiding the police to apprehend the kidnapers in a way that combined iron nerve with a general's strategy. The unfortunate thing was that Judy's mind kept dodging off on bypaths of its own—lanes with no end, but with frequent, unexpected turnings. And around each turn she would come face to face with Shadow and Sambo or with Boy and Brother. She could see them as clearly as though they were here in the room with her, fat black bodies wriggling, tails awag, innocent eyes unaware that they were star performers in a mystery which fascinated Judy even more than the one between the pages of her book.

Where, she kept wondering, were Boy and Brother now? Back safely in their pen or wandering up to some farmer's door for a begged breakfast? Suppose, as Mr. Matthews had suggested, they became thoroughly terrified, and simply cowered in the underbrush for days, trembling and wretched? Always, lying in bed, Judy allowed her imagination full rein. She could even bring tears to her eyes, without half trying, as she envisioned two small puppies alone in a menacing world, lost like—like the Babes in the Wood.

Judy put herself in the dogs' place. She crouched,

chilled and shivering, against the packed wet leaves of a thicket while the storm rolled and roared overhead. She pawed her way through a tangle of brambles, which scratched her tender skin under her drenched black fur. Thorns tore at her long ears like sharp, clutching fingernails. Judy's hands, under her head, were tensely locked. Poor babies, she thought. Poor, poor babies. Alone in the night and afraid.

Judy blew her nose again and looked at the crawling clock hands. She wished Jeff would hurry.

Still, by now, Boy and Brother might be back home. Judy sighed and sailed off on another, less heart-rending tack. She might be worrying needlessly. By now the pups may well have been dried, brushed, and fed a substantial breakfast, she tried to tell herself. But she couldn't be sure. She wished she knew.

The terrace door banged and there was a muffled sound of voices below. Judy couldn't wait. "Jeff!" she called.

Her mother's voice answered. "It isn't Jeff, Judy. It's Lynn. Would you like her to come up?"

"Oh, yes, Mommy! Please."

The voices went on, more distinct now, and the things they were saying seemed maddeningly inconsequential to the girl in bed.

"You're not afraid of catching Judy's cold, dear?"

"Not in the least, Mrs. Sutherland. I'm awfully sorry, though, that it was sort of my fault—at least the fault of the dogs . . ."

"Are they back, Lynn?" shouted Judy.

Lynn replied on her way upstairs. "Not a sign of them," she said in a voice that contained a certain surprise. "I tramped all through the woods again this morning and called and called. I'm here now to use your phone, if I may. I think I ought to call the police and report that they are lost, don't you?"

"Of course!" Judy said, then chuckled. "The police force will be seeing black cocker spaniels in its sleep."

Lynn looked a little dismayed. "If you think I oughtn't—"

"Don't be silly," Judy grinned. "I think it's the only thing to do."

After Lynn had telephoned she came back and sat on the dressing-table stool. "I went back to the farm and down to the highway and even up to the old quarry," she continued. "I don't see how they could have wandered much farther away."

"Don't worry. They'll turn up." Judy tried, ineffectually, to stifle another sneeze.

Lynn was at once all contrition. "Your cold! Here I've been so wrapped up in my own affairs I never said a word!"

Judy waved her hand. "A cold's not interesting. The pups are."

But Lynn had to offer her condolences. She felt very regretful and responsible. She was still telling Judy how sorry she was when Jeff came upstairs, two at a time.

"Hi!" he said when he saw Lynn. "I was just going up to your place. Are they back?"

Lynn shook her head regretfully. "The paint's dry though," she added. "It looks wonderful."

Judy thought it probably looked a little short of wonderful, but she was glad Lynn was pleased. When she got up and around again, she promised herself, she would tackle the problem of the furniture. Jeff flopped down on the foot of his sister's bed and the three chatted for a while. Then Lynn left, promising to keep them posted in case the puppies should turn up, either arriving under their own steam or found by the police.

When Lynn had gone Jeff came back to Judy's room with a couple of new magazines and the local weekly newspaper, which he'd picked up for her downtown. "It's sort of funny they haven't turned up, don't you think?" he asked thoughtfully, the dogs still on his mind.

Before Judy could reply Mamam came into the room from the front of the house, her crocheting clutched in one hand, her despised cane in the other. "Who hasn't turned up?" she asked sharply. Then her eyes darted from Jeff to Judy. "You don't look well, child. Keep covered up."

She eased herself carefully down to the window seat, at a safe distance from Judy's "germs," and made Jeff get up from the foot of the bed and out of harm's way also. Then she fixed her crochet hook firmly in

the piece of bedspread she was crocheting and said,
"Well, tell me about it."

Judy started. She described how she'd run out to
the pen to find the door open and the pups gone; how
she was sure, from a noise in the underbrush, that
they'd taken to the woods; how she'd pursued and
called their names against the noise of the whipping
wind, only to land ignominiously with her head on a
rock where Jeff and Lynn had found her.

Then Jeff took up the tale, fully repaid by
Mamam's "Oh's," "Ah's," and "My land!'s" for the
dramatic fervor of his delivery. But when the twins got
right down to it, as far as the mystery was concerned
the chase through the storm didn't contribute a thing
to the sum total of evidence.

"Looks as though Matthews was going to end up
with no dogs at all, let alone the right ones," Mamam
commented with a shake of her head when Jeff had
finished. It began to look that way to Judy too.

She lay and thought for a long time after Jeff left
the room. Mamam crocheted industriously, humming
in a low monotone but not attempting to carry on a
connected conversation. Judy glanced at her from time
to time affectionately. She wasn't like most elderly
ladies, always talking, talking about the past.

Once during the morning she made a suggestion.
"Jeff ought to check on the rest of the people Mike
Matthews works for, just to be sure," she said.

"Sure about what?" Judy had forgotten the original plan.

"Sure that none of them gave him two cocker pups."

She said the same thing to Jeff, when he came back to report that the swimming pool was still too low for use. "I'll do it this afternoon," he promised. "I know who they all are now."

Neither Judy nor Mamam, however, believed that much would come of this move. They were neither of them surprised when Jeff came home about four o'clock to say that none of the gardener's other employers were doggy people, except one man who kept an enormous great Dane confined to a pen at the back of his house.

Judy, however, had something interesting to report. Glancing through the suburban weekly she had run across an announcement that was provocative. On the coming Saturday, at a house called "The Hedges," the Schuylkill Valley Kennel Club was holding a match show.

At first it hadn't meant a thing to Judy. Her eyes had run over the item idly, then come back. "Mamam," she asked, "what's a match show?"

"Match?" Mamam frowned. "What are you talking about?"

"It must have something to do with dogs," Judy said. "It's being held by a kennel club."

Mrs. Sutherland, coming into the room with a tall glass of fruit juice for Judy, heard the last remarks.

"I know what a match show is," she said, as though she were faintly surprised at her own astuteness. "Nancy Rogers was talking about one just this morning. Being held somewhere near here, I think. It's an informal sort of dog show, for puppies and young dogs who haven't been shown a great deal. It's almost like a tryout, according to Nancy. Why?"

"There's one being held at a house called 'The Hedges,'" Judy answered.

"That's the Clark Jameson place, over Radnor way," nodded her mother.

"I wonder," Judy murmured. "Can anybody go?"

Mrs. Sutherland, plumping up the pillows on Judy's bed, said: "I don't know. I suppose so. I could ask Nancy. She's going to look at a collie pup she's interested in for Bill. Maybe you'd better not mention that though. It's for his birthday and maybe she intends it for a surprise."

Judy laughed. Her mother was no keeper of secrets. "I'll be careful," she promised. "But will you do something for me? Will you see if Mrs. Rogers would be willing to take Jeff and me along?"

Mrs. Sutherland looked at her daughter curiously. She'd thought the twins' sudden interest in dogs was personal, not academic. "If your cold's all gone . . ." she said vaguely.

"It will be all gone. Honestly, mommy, it will!"

"All right," Mrs. Sutherland agreed.

From the window seat Mamam's thin voice piped

up, "If there should be enough room left over for an old lady, I'd kind of like to go too."

As the week wore slowly on, Judy was glad that she had something ahead to get well for. The cold was persistent, and her mother kept her in bed until noon every day. In the afternoons Lynn took to wandering down, to sit under the cherry tree and talk. Not a word had beeen heard of Boy or Brother, though the police had felt sure they would turn up at some private house in the neighborhood.

"Maybe it just wasn't in the cards for you to have cocker spaniels," Judy said sorrowfully.

"Maybe it wasn't," Lynn agreed, but her eyes were dark with dismay. "I don't know what Daddy is ever . . ." she started, then bit her lip.

"What were you going to say?"

"Nothing," Lynn shook her head. "It wasn't important."

But Judy had a feeling that it was very important indeed. If only she had Lynn's confidence!

15

"WHEN I WAS A LITTLE GIRL," STOUT MRS.
Rogers was explaining to Jeff, who sat beside her on
the front seat of the Pontiac, "my best friend's father
used to breed collies. He took us to a lot of dog shows
and taught us to recognize the points of several different breeds. It was quite an education."

In the back seat Judy, bouncing along beside Mamam, whose bonnet sat rather tipsily on her erect
head, tried to keep her mind on the conversation. She
was glad that Bill Rogers stood a good chance of getting a collie for his birthday. She supposed a collie
was a boy's dog, though for herself she'd prefer a
spaniel—a coal-black cocker with liquid eyes like
Shadow, Sambo, Boy, or Brother. She would have
settled instantly for any one of the four.

Nervously she smoothed the skirt of her white
sharkskin dress and glanced down at the new red san-
dals on her bare brown feet. She hoped she looked all

• 179 •

right. She hadn't known exactly what people might wear to a match show.

The meaning of the term was still vague in Judy's mind. She was only sure that puppies would be shown, and that might mean—just possibly!—that the Gross Point Kennels would be represented by their two most promising males. Jeff and Mamam both apparently shared her desire for another look at Shadow and Sambo. Just what they expected to gain from this neither they nor Judy quite knew. It just seemed that any sleuth interested in the black spaniel mystery couldn't afford to miss such a chance.

"In a match show," Jeff was saying to Mrs. Rogers, "are there ribbons and prizes, like a dog show?"

"That's right. Except that it's unprofessional and that no dog who has received his championship can be shown. This is an all-breed match, you understand, and there will be puppy classes as well as novice and open."

It all sounded rather sophisticated and quite unintelligible to Judy, though Jeff nodded his head as though he understood perfectly. Judy glanced at Mamam, and Mamam grinned and winked. Then she shook her head to indicate that she didn't understand either. Judy sighed and tucked her arm under her companion's black-and-white flowered silk sleeve. She guessed that there were some women who were bright about such things and some women who were dumb.

Somehow Mamam had made it seem all right to feel a little stupid.

Slowing down, Mrs. Rogers turned into a straight road bounded by an eight-foot hedge along which a number of cars were parked. "High hedges. You can see where the place gets its name," she said.

The car turned in at an open gate and followed a straight drive up to a rambling colonial house with broad lawns spreading on all sides. Station wagons and cars were parked in the garage area and pulled onto the grass at the side of the drive. People and dogs were everywhere—in the cars, on the lawn, on the porch of the house. Under the strong afternoon sun everything looked bright and vigorous and a little confusing. Judy began to wonder whether Mamam might not find this melee too tiring. She couldn't see any place where an elderly lady might sit down.

"Now don't you worry about me." Reading Judy's thoughts, Mamam reached out to pat her hand with an abrupt little tap. "If I get tired, I can always come right back here to the car."

A middle-aged man in a white linen sports coat walked over to the car and collected the admission fees. "Showing any dogs?" he asked Mrs. Rogers.

She shook her head. "Just spectators."

"The rings are around back of the house," he volunteered.

Mrs. Rogers and Judy went ahead, Jeff following more slowly with Mamam. Several people looked at the old lady curiously, Jeff noticed. A person of her age was apparently a rarity at such an event.

But Mamam herself was unperturbed by their stares. She stepped briskly along, darting quick glances to left and right, as interested as the twins in the color and activity of the scene surrounding her.

Mrs. Rogers, quite naturally, wanted to go at once to the ring where collies would be judged. "There's a young pup from the Post Kennels I have my eye on," she explained to Judy. "I intend to buy him if he does well today."

They rounded the corner of the house as she spoke, and before them stretched a full acre of lawn which swept down to a pool at its base. Here there were even more dogs and people than in the front of the house, but to Judy's relief they seemed considerably more orderly, chatting in groups, parading their dogs, or gathering on the outskirts of six roped-off squares where the judging would take place. Around the edges of the squares were wooden chairs, supplemented by lawn furniture and benches from the terrace, which had been given over to a sandwich and soft-drink bar, set up under a striped awning.

Mrs. Rogers stopped a woman wearing an arm band with JUDGE printed in gold on it. "Where are collies being shown?" she asked.

Judy wanted to ask about cockers too, but before she could get up courage the judge had answered her hostess's question and walked away. She kept a sharp lookout, however, as she wove with Mrs. Rogers in and out of the groups dotting the lawn, and almost tripped over the leash of a low-slung dachshund as she spotted a black cocker puppy that looked, for a moment, like Shadow or Sambo. But the woman on the other end of the leash was wrong. She was talking to a friend in a voice that carried distinctly to Judy. "I consider this one of the finest pups I've ever bred," she said.

Jeff, with his left hand tucked under Mamam's arm, was interested in the activity within the various rings. Judging, in some cases, had already started, and handlers and owners were parading their dogs before men and women whose discerning eyes followed every movement of the animals on the leads. In one ring a judge was sliding expert hands along the shoulders and back of an Irish setter. In another, on a wooden table knocked together out of rough boards, an owner fixed the forelegs of a beagle so that he would show to advantage. Every snatch of conversation that reached Jeff's ears concerned dogs. Every onlooker seemed to have eyes for some particular breed, to the exclusion of all others. Jeff knew that Mrs. Rogers would be concentrating on the collies and he also knew that Judy, who by now was trotting along a few steps behind Bill's mother, would be agog with impatience to break away and seek out the ring where spaniels would be judged.

But first Jeff wanted to ask Mrs. Rogers some questions. He wanted to find out what the various ribbons meant, what classes would be judged, what prizes might be given. He felt that to appreciate the contest he must understand its rules, and he was more willing than Judy to take time to learn.

It was natural, therefore, that Judy should fall back with Mamam, and that Jeff should join Mrs. Rogers when she paused near a group of collies waiting on the outskirts of one of the rings. Judy, at the same moment, spotted three cockers being walked on a split leash by a man in a chauffeur's uniform. Her eyes followed the dogs' progress until it ended at a roped-off square some distance to the left. "Let's walk over there!" she suggested at once. "Mrs. Rogers will never miss us. I'll find you a place to sit down and then I'll walk back and tell her where we'll be."

Mamam agreed readily. She was panting a little by now, and the thought of sitting down seemed good. When Judy helped her to ease herself into a collapsible wooden chair she gave a short grunt of satisfaction. This was a comfortable vantage point. "I'll be all right here," she said.

At the entrance to the ring, as both she and Judy could see, several men and women with very young puppies on leads were standing in a haphazard group. The puppies—blond, red, parti-colored, and black— were dancing and straining at their leads, anxious to investigate each other, excited by the strange smells and sounds that greeted them on every side.

"Puppies. Dogs. Three to six months," called a fair-

haired man with eyeglasses from inside the ring. "Numbers 73, 76, 59, and 80."

The dogs, with their handlers, filed through the opening. One puppy was reluctant, straining against the leash. Another was playful, jumping against his master's legs. The spectators smiled. "Puppies always amuse me because they don't know how to behave in a ring," Judy heard the woman sitting next to Mamam say.

But once Judy had made sure that no Gross Point cockers were in the group her attention wandered. Suppose Mr. Gross weren't showing today after all!

Her eyes searched the side lines. It was easier to look for a big red-haired man than for a black cocker pup. There were half a dozen black cockers wandering about on leads, and from a distance one looked very like another. But the owner of the Gross Point Kennels was nowhere about.

"I'd better go get Jeff," Judy said, after a minute.

She felt that to share her disappointment might lessen it.

"That's right," said Mamam, shrewdly discerning Judy's need. "I'll keep watch here."

Jeff was engrossed in Mrs. Rogers' explanation of match-show routine when Judy came up, but he allowed himself to be wheedled away. "We have some friends who own cockers," he explained to his hostess. "You don't mind . . ."

"Not a bit," Mrs. Rogers said casually. "You can look me up later."

The minute Judy had her twin alone she said, "They're showing puppies, but I don't think Shadow and Sambo are here." Her mouth turned down at the corners and she looked very woebegone.

"What age pups?" asked Jeff at once, proud in his newly acquired store of information.

Judy tried to think. "Three to six months, I think he said."

"They're just the babies," replied Jeff lightly. "Shadow and Sambo are well over six months old by now."

"Of course!" Judy gave a short, hopeful skip. Her spirits lifted again.

By the time they arrived at the ring where sporting dogs were being shown, a group of female puppies were being paraded past the judge. Mamam, paying no attention to the showing, beckoned to them at once.

"Isn't that Young Art over there, talking to the woman in red? I can't quite see . . ."

Judy's and Jeff's eyes followed the nod of Mamam's head. Mr. Gross was indeed standing with his broad back to the ring, in conversation with a woman who had a parti-colored spaniel on a lead. But each of the twins saw at once that he had both hands in his jacket pockets. Neither Shadow, Sambo, nor any other Gross Point cocker accompanied him. For the second time in ten minutes Judy's eager hopes were dashed.

Jeff tried to be more optimistic. "Maybe he has his dogs in the car," he suggested.

"Maybe," Judy said doubtfully. She slid into the chair now vacant next to Mamam. "That's Mr. Gross all right," she said, "but he doesn't have any dogs with him."

"Hmph!" Mamam muttered. "Why not?"

It was a question none of them could answer. After all, Judy tried to console herself, it was just a *chance*. They had no right to be too disappointed. After all . . .

The judge, a wiry, sharp-eyed man with freckles, was handing out ribbons. A girl with a red puppy nodded as she received a pink one and the bystanders clapped.

"Pink is for first prize," Jeff whispered to Judy. "It's like a blue ribbon in a point show." He sounded almost as erudite as Mrs. Rogers herself.

The judge passed out a yellow ribbon and a green, then retired to a table at the side of the ring to examine a chart. The handlers led their puppies out of the area and the man with the eyeglasses came forward and called: "Puppies. Dogs. Six to twelve months. Numbers 82, 84, 88, 89, and 90."

Idly Judy watched the dogs come into the ring, her mind on other things. Then, suddenly, Mamam grabbed her arm. "Isn't that Young Art's kennelman?"

Judy followed the direction of her glance, but she saw, not the man, but the dog on the leash that he held. "Jeff!" she cried softly. "Look!"

For some reason she was reminded of the first time she'd seen Shadow and Sambo, prancing down the road like cocksure young gallants, without a care in the world. The black dog at which she now looked had the same gay carriage, the same high-held head. The other puppies sniffed and frisked, lagged or bounded ahead, but this pup walked smartly, tail wagging just a little, legs moving in a smooth rhythm. He walked proudly, like a showman to the manner born. He was as outstanding among his competitors as a purebred dog amid a group of mongrels. From the side lines a murmured "Oh!" hung in the air.

"Which is it?" Jeff asked. "Shadow or Sambo?"

"I don't know," Judy whispered back, "but isn't he beautiful?"

He was indeed. He was large for his age and he circled the ring once, then twice, before the judge halted the handlers and instructed them, one by one, to bring their pups to the table, where he examined their bite, their teeth, their foot pads, their conformation. The dog stood quietly when the kennelman lifted him up, not even turning his head when the judge ran his hands down his flanks. The spectators were watching the pup closely, talking among themselves, and on the far side of the ring Judy could see Mr. Gross following the black pup with his eyes, a smile that contained just a touch of arrogance curving his thick lips.

No one, least of all Judy, was surprised when the judge handed the pink ribbon to the black pup's handler. "That was a walkaway," the girl heard a voice behind her remark.

Jeff looked at his twin and nodded in agreement. "But where d'you suppose his brother is?" he asked.

"I can't imagine," Judy murmured, twisting in her chair. "Do you think maybe he's sick?"

Mamam came up with a reasonable explanation. "Maybe Young Art just didn't want to pit one against the other," she said.

But Judy frowned, puzzled and a little worried. It didn't seem right for Shadow and Sambo to be apart.

Then the activity in the ring claimed her attention. "Novice. Dogs," the bespectacled gentleman was saying. "Numbers 94, 107, 97, 98, 103, 89."

"Eighty-nine!" said Jeff, squeezing Judy's shoulder. "Hey! That's our pup again."

The black dog was competing against an older, steadier group now. Many of them had points to their credit from regular shows. It was a situation in which many a pup would have shown up as awkward and undeveloped, yet the Gross Point entrant paraded with the same easy arrogance that he had shown in the ring before.

The judge, Judy noticed, was paying special attention to the black pup and to a red-and-white dog, heavily coated and beautifully marked, whose broad muzzle and full eyes made him outstanding. He asked the handlers to bring the two dogs forward and he compared their conformation in a leisurely fashion. Then he watched them walk, coming toward him, going away from him. Judy watched too, wondering what was going on inside the judge's head. At the far side of the ring she could see Mr. Gross, equally intent.

"A puppy'd have to be pretty good, wouldn't he," she whispered to Jeff, "to win against all these older dogs?"

"Yep. I guess!" Then Jeff added, "Mr. Gross wouldn't be showing him, I'll bet, unless he stands a fair chance."

Mamam nodded. "Young Art's smart. Nobody's ever said Young Art isn't smart."

Judy was watching the judge. It seemed to take him an especially long time to make up his mind. He crossed the grass to the table, picked up the chart and consulted with his assistant as he made notations on it. Then he took the three ribbons and started over to where the handlers now waited with their dogs. For an agonizing moment Judy thought he was going first toward the stout woman who held the red-and-white fellow, but then he swerved and handed the pink ribbon, with a short nod of congratulation, to the Gross Point kennelman.

A gasp went up from the crowd. People clapped, and Judy joined them. "Oh, I'm glad!" she cried. She was glad for the puppy's sake. She only wished it could have been Lynn or her father on the other end of the leash. Her young voice rang out in a higher key than the adult voices near her, and several spectators turned to smile at the excited girl. Even Artemus Gross, coming around to receive the pink ribbon from his handler, heard her spontaneous cheer. He glanced at Judy in surprised recognition, then at Mamam and Jeff.

Mamam apprehended the man's look and nodded. Mr. Gross, in turn, bowed politely and smiled. Then a stout woman and her dog stepped between them, but in the moment they had been face to face Judy thought she had detected a shadow of fright behind the surprise in the kennel owner's eyes.

For a time Mr. Gross was surrounded. Friends and acquaintances came up to speak to him and to admire the dog his kennelman still held. Fragments of congratulatory remarks reached the twins' ears. "Magnificent head . . . splendid carriage . . ." Then a reporter with a notebook and pencil asked, "What do you call him, sir?"

"King Cole," Judy heard Mr. Gross reply, and she looked at Jeff in puzzled dismay before she realized that of course this was the dog's kennel name.

"What about his littermates?" a breeder asked, and Mr. Gross hesitated just an instant before he replied, "This is the best."

Jeff leaned over Judy's shoulder. "That's a lot of hooey," he muttered. "Shadow and Sambo are so much alike *we* can't tell 'em apart."

Judy was about to reply when she realized that Mr. Gross was coming toward Mamam. "Good afternoon, Mrs. Whiteman," he said cordially. "This is an unexpected place to find a lady your age."

Mamam immediately bridled. "You think so?" she said. "I went to a horse race last spring." But she softened the pique in her voice with a sly grin.

Mr. Gross laughed and responded, then waited while his father's old sparring partner introduced her incongruously young companions. "Judith and Jeffrey Sutherland, my godchildren," she said as though she knew nothing of their past encounters.

To the twins' surprise, Mr. Gross greeted them very graciously and stood talking about the show and the success of his black puppy as though they were all the best of friends. His attitude bewildered Judy. She even began to wonder whether she might not have misjudged him. He seemed very jovial and pleasant indeed.

Jeff, she could tell, was equally confused. As the

conversation progressed Judy had a hunch that it was on the tip of his tongue to ask about the other black puppy, but just at the moment when such a question might have seemed natural Mrs. Rogers joined them with a young collie in tow. The conversation was turned at once away from cocker spaniels, and after Judy and Jeff had admired Bill's birthday present with all the enthusiasm at their command their hostess suggested that it might be time to start home.

Judy, glancing at Mamam, agreed. Although the little lady was still game, excitement and exertion had tired her. She readily accepted Judy's help in getting to her feet, and when Artemus Gross offered his arm she took it without question.

On the way back to the car Mr. Gross walked on one side of Mamam, Judy on the other. Jeff, astonished by the kennel owner's unexpected solicitude, went ahead with Mrs. Rogers and the collie pup. Every now and then Mamam stopped and rested for a few seconds, at the same time keeping up a spirited conversation with her escort. It was during one of these rests, as they neared the parking area, that the Gross Point kennelman and the black pup crossed their path.

Mamam's eyes followed the puppy dreamily as he was lifted into the station wagon by his handler. "That's a fine-looking dog," she told her companion. "I only remember one other dog that took my fancy as much. It wasn't a black dog though. It was one of those light tan ones. But it had the same short body, the same elegant way of walking. Maybe you remember her?" she asked Mr. Gross guilelessly. "Gay Lady, she was called—one of Amelia Carstairs' dogs."

Judy hoped her face didn't betray her amazement. At the same time she thought that Mamam's apparent innocence might fool anyone except herself or Jeff, might even fool Artemus Gross. Guardedly she looked up at the man from under her long eyelashes.

Mamam was nodding her head, as though bemused. "Yes, there's quite a resemblance," she was rambling on. "*Quite* a resemblance. Except for the color, of course."

"You don't say!" Mr. Gross murmured, in the tone successful men sometimes use when humoring old ladies. "That's very interesting. Of course," he added with a smile, "the heyday of the Carstairs' kennels was rather before my time."

They walked on after a minute and Mr. Gross handed Mamam into the car with considerate gallantry. He joked for a moment with Mrs. Rogers, then said good-by to the twins and waited to wave the party off before he turned to walk back to his station wagon.

On the back seat Judy could contain herself only until they made the turn at the gate. "You never even saw Gay Lady!" she scolded Mamam in a shocked whisper.

"Who says so?" Mamam looked offended and indignant.

Judy wasn't abashed. "Mamam, you know . . ."

Suddenly Mamam grinned. She reached out and patted Judy's hand. "I didn't say I'd actually seen Gay Lady. I only said I knew her, and I feel that I do. I didn't tell a fib, either, so you needn't look like that. When people get to be eighty, child, they ought to be allowed some peculiarities. Now hush!"

Judy obediently subsided. She lay back against the cushions of the car and let her mind drift while Mamam fell into an untroubled doze. One thing still concerned her—the whereabouts of the other black puppy. She wanted to ask Jeff if he thought it was possible that he might already have been sold. But Jeff, up front, was busy being agreeable to Mrs. Rogers, and the opportunity, even later, never seemed to come. It was a question Judy took to bed with her—a question that was answered the next day in a rather astonishing way.

16

THE LETTER WAS
there, stuck in the screen
door, when the Sutherlands
got home from church the next morning. It was addressed to Mrs. Jennie Whiteman in an aggressive masculine hand. It had no address, no stamp. Country fashion, it had just been dropped off at the house.

"Land," said Mamam, "who could be writing to me?"

Jeff pulled the envelope, heavy and unsealed, out of the door and handed it to her. Mamam just stood there, fingering the expensive paper and turning it over in her hand.

"Aren't you going to open it?" Judy asked impatiently.

"When I get my spectacles. There's plenty of time. This is the Sabbath, child—no day to hurry things."

Deliberately she mounted the steps to the house, went into the living room, removed the two old-fashioned hatpins that held her bonnet precariously in place, laid the headgear on top of the high chest of drawers, and walked over to sit down in the Boston rocker that stood by the big bay window. Judy followed her, fidgeting.

"Where are your specs, Mamam? I'll get them."

"They might be on the bureau, or they might be with my fancywork, or again they could be on the kitchen cabinet behind the sugar bowl. I guess you'll have to look."

Judy looked, racing upstairs and down. They were in none of these possible places, but she found them at last, tucked half under a vase of roses on the deep dining room window sill. "Now hurry!" she urged. "Maybe somebody's asking you to a party."

But it was an invitation of a vastly different kind that greeted Mamam's eyes when she opened the envelope. At the top of the single sheet was a crest engraved in maroon ink, and under it the scrawled salutation, "My dear Mrs. Whiteman . . ."

Peering over the tops of her glasses, Mamam deciphered the message slowly, reading it aloud to Judy:

"Since you were so good as to admire my black puppy, King Cole, at the show at 'The Hedges' yesterday, I am wondering if you wouldn't care to accept his brother as a gift? You will remember the other dog, I am sure, from having seen him when you paid me a call less than a fortnight ago. He is a fine little fellow, affectionate, obedient, and gay. Unfortunately, since he has been raised in a kennel, he is not yet house-broken, but I am sure this will offer you no special problem. I feel certain that he would make a splendid companion for an elderly lady, living alone. Think it over for a few days, if you care to; then let me know.

> "Yours in sincere regard,
>
> "Artemus J. Gross, Jr."

"It don't make sense." Mamam's grammar deserted her as she wagged her head from side to side and stared at Judy. "What's Young Art offering me a thousand-dollar puppy for? It don't make sense."

It didn't make sense to Judy, either, nor to Jeff. To Mr. and Mrs. Sutherland too, it seemed an incredibly generous gesture.

"Screwy," was Jeff's pronouncement.

"Extraordinary!" was his father's. "Why, Artemus Gross scarcely knows you, Aunt Jen, except through your association with his parents." He chuckled. "And that, if I remember, was none too friendly."

"Old Art was no good," Mamam retorted at once. She stared down at the letter she held in one shaky hand and idly fingered the crest. "Anyways, what would I want with a puppy at my age? I don't need a companion. I need peace of mind. And I can't see an unhousebroken, rambunctious puppy giving me that."

Judy caught Jeff's eye. She privately thought that peace of mind was far from what Mamam most desired. Jeff, she could tell, was equally amused at the phrase, but he didn't smile. "You could take it out on a lead," he suggested.

"And get pulled off my feet? I have enough trouble getting around as it is!" Mamam was suddenly belligerent, as though she were annoyed rather than flattered that Artemus Gross had offered her the dog at all.

The Sutherlands all laughed, and Mrs. Sutherland said: "Now don't get edgy, Mamam. A man doesn't think of all those things. I can't understand why Mr. Gross would want you to have one of his best puppies, but if he does—well, he does. And whether you want to accept it or not, I think it was a very nice offer for him to make."

Mamam snorted and changed the subject. "Look at this crest here!" she said. "Just look! Makes about as much sense as me having a puppy dog under foot. Old Art Gross never had any family tree he could trace back farther'n the scrawny poplar in his front yard."

But by the time dinner was finished she had come around, generally speaking, to Mrs. Sutherland's point of view. Try as she would, she could fathom no nefarious reason for such a gesture on Young Art's part, and since it was Sunday and a ripe, balmy day it occurred to her that in some instances the sins of the father might not always be visited on the son.

She said as much to Jeff as he helped her down the flagstone steps from the terrace for a turn about the garden to look at "Sheila's flowers." "Your mother may be right," she mused as she knocked a Japanese beetle off a scarlet rosebud with the tip of her cane. "If Young Art is simply being good-hearted I have no cause to revile him, whether I want the puppy or not."

"Whether you want it or not, I wish you'd take it," said Jeff.

"Take it?" Mamam's voice shrilled in surprise. "Land, child, d'you think I'm crazy?"

Jeff shook his head, grinning. "No, but I think Mr. Gross is, to want to give away such a valuable pup. Either something's happened to the dog that makes him useless for showing—and that would explain why he wasn't in the ring with King Cole at 'High Hedges' —or Mr. Gross has gone completely haywire. No matter how rich a man is, I can't believe he'll just—poof! —give away a thousand bucks."

Mamam, unexpectedly, bridled. "You know, Jeffrey," she said, "it's entirely possible that we could all have been mistaken about Young Art."

Judy, coming up to them, struck an attitude. "Behind that monogrammed shirt front may beat a heart of gold."

"How do you know it's monogrammed?" Jeff asked.

"I don't. I just suspect."

"Well, *I* suspect the heart is made of brass," Jeff retorted.

"Now, now!" Mamam scolded, shaking her cane. "We must be fair. That's very important. Colonel

Primrose is never influenced by friendship in solving a case. We must try to be open-minded."

Jeff looked at Judy and quirked his mouth at one corner knowingly. "I think she's gone over to the enemy," he said in an elaborate stage whisper.

Mamam stamped her cane. "Nothing of the kind. I'm just trying not to be biased, that's all."

"Then," said Jeff with dubious logic, "you *will* accept the puppy as a gift?"

"I haven't said I would and I haven't said I won't. I'll think it over."

The twins had to be satisfied with that. In their own minds they worked out the details of how the situation could be handled. Mamam would thank Mr. Gross very much and say she'd be pleased to have the puppy. Then, while she was staying with the Sutherlands, Judy and Jeff could take over its responsibility. Just before she was ready to go home she could decide that the dog would be too much for her after all, and call Mr. Gross to tell him so. In the back of her mind Judy nourished a weak hope that Mr. Gross might then offer the pup to Jeff and herself. She didn't mention this to Jeff, because she knew he would hoot at such a possibility. But privately she hugged it to her. There was just a ghost of a chance. . . . Maybe, after all, Artemus Gross might really be a sheep in wolf's clothing.

Of course, as they told Mamam, the main object

of getting the pup into their hands was to satisfy their curiosity concerning the missing dewclaws.

"And what's that going to prove now?" Mamam asked astutely.

"Now?" Judy didn't understand.

"Now that the other pair of dogs are gone."

The twins thought it over. The case for Lynn, strung originally on a thin strand indeed, seemed to be torn apart completely.

"I think," said Judy slowly, "that we should make another effort to get Lynn's confidence. She's worried and she's frightened about something. I'm sure of that. If she'd only tell us how she got the puppies!"

"It might be interesting," Mamam mused aloud, "to see how Lynn would react if you were to tell her Young Art has offered me one of his dogs."

"It might," Jeff agreed. "It might even persuade her to break down and tell us all." He turned to Judy. "Let's walk up the hill and have a try."

Lynn was arranging petunias in a bowl on the living-room table when the twins arrived. Their deep purples and whites were effective against the cold yellow of the painted walls and Judy thought with a thrill of accomplishment that the room did look a lot better, in spite of the ugly furniture. "The kitchen curtains are up too," said Lynn. "Want to see them?"

After the brave red-and-white checks had been duly admired Jeff launched his thunderbolt. "What do you think?" he asked. "Mr. Gross has offered to give Mamam one of the black puppies."

Lynn's eyes widened and her lower jaw unconsciously dropped. "He never . . ." she said.

"It's true though." Judy backed up Jeff. "It's all right there in a note that came this morning while we were at church."

Lynn clenched her hands until the knuckles showed white. "But why?" she cried, her eyes growing dark. "Why? Why?"

"That's what we hoped you'd know," Jeff began.

"I? I haven't the slightest idea!" Lynn's voice rose sharply, then became worried. "Unless something's happened to the puppy. Unless he's been hurt. So that he'd be no good . . ." She broke off abruptly and a mask slid over her face.

Judy tried to break through the sudden reserve. "Look, Lynn," she said gently. "We want to help you, Jeff and I. But you keep too much from us. We can't help you if you won't tell us anything. Surely you can see that!"

Lynn shook her head. Her eyes filled with unshed tears. "I'm sorry," she said, just above a whisper. "I can't."

So the twins came away from the Matthews' feeling that they hadn't accomplished a thing. They reported the conversation in detail to Mamam expecting her to get nothing from it. But when they came to Lynn's suggestion that the puppy offered as a gift might have been hurt the old lady sat up very straight.

"Hurt?" she said. "I'll just find out. I'll accept Young Art's offer all right. I'll call him in the morning first thing."

But the first thing on Monday morning something happened to distract the twins. Jeff had just clattered downstairs to breakfast and Judy was still sleepily braiding her hair when Lynn dashed down the hill in a frenzy of excitement.

Judy saw her first in the mirror which faced the window of her room. She crossed the floor and tapped on the screen. "Hi, Lynn! What's up?" she called just as Jeff banged out of the kitchen door.

"Up in the woods or somewhere," Lynn cried breathlessly, "I can hear dogs barking. They sound exactly like Boy and Brother. You know the way they'd war-whoop when they tired of the pen! But I can't find them. I've called and I've searched. I was wondering—could you—come help?"

"We haven't had any breakfast," said Jeff dubiously, but Judy cut in.

"Of course we'll come. Jeff, grab a banana and a piece of toast for me. We can eat them on the way. I'll be right down!"

Dew still glistened on the long fronds of the field grass and the air smelled fresh and clean as Judy followed Lynn up the hill. Jeff trailed along laconically, still thinking about the bacon and eggs he had deserted, but his twin was filled with early morning exhilaration. She strained her ears to hear a distant bark.

"I was out feeding the chickens," Lynn explained as they hurried along. "I called them the way I always do—'Here chick-chick-chick'—and all of a sudden I heard it, a noise between a bark and a howl. It sounded exactly like Boy. But when I called nothing happened. I went up to the edge of the woods and it seemed louder. Then it was repeated and it seemed very far away. I worked through the woods for a bit, but I couldn't seem to trace it at all."

Jeff ate the last of his banana and threw away the skin.

"I wish we'd hear it again!" Judy puffed.

They went straight back to the edge of the woods and Lynn called, making a megaphone of her hands. "Boy! Brother! Here, puppies!"

There was an answering bark, quite distinct, then another. Then a whole series of short barks seemed to topple over each other, fading away finally into distant silence.

Suddenly Jeff laughed.

Judy turned to look at him curiously. He looked like a cat who had swallowed a canary. "Well?" she said.

"I don't know whether it's the pups or not," he said ungrammatically, "but I know where those barks are coming from."

"Where?" Lynn asked.

"The old quarry hole of course. Those last barks were echoes." As Jeff delivered this pronouncement he looked from one of his companions to the other with an unspoken sentence on his lips. "Sometimes girls can be so dumb!"

They all knew the path that led to the quarry hole. It was on the fringe of the woods, quite close to the highway, screened from the road only by a sheltering hedge, about fifty yards wide, of bushes and trees. Running, they skirted the Matthews' yard and hurried along the ridge of the hill until a footpath turned sharply to the right. Jeff, faster than the girls, dodged into the cover of the trees first, Lynn right on his heels and Judy, whose leather-soled moccasins kept slipping on the wet grass, puffing along behind.

"Boy!" Lynn called again. "Brother!"

The answering barks were close by now. "They *are* there!" Judy cried, though Jeff and Lynn were too far ahead to hear her.

When she reached the quarry hole, a slow third, both Jeff and Lynn were on their knees, peering over, and Lynn was saying, in a puzzled tone, "How d'you ever suppose they got down there?"

Judy dropped to the ground too, and crawled forward to crane her neck over the ledge. The quarry hole was not large, but it was deep, and against the cut-shaped curve of its walls scrambled two frantic black cocker pups.

"How we'll get them out is more to the point,"

growled Jeff. "It's not so hard to get down, but I can't see scrambling up those rocks with a squirming dog that weighs a good fifteen pounds."

Judy, as yet, was unperturbed by this problem. She followed Lynn's lead and called: "Here, Boy! Here, Brother!" to be rewarded by more furious barking than ever and mad, ineffectual leaps into the air.

"Last night," Lynn said, "I thought I heard them barking—in a dream—"

"Look here," Jeff cut in. "Will you gals talk sense? We've—got—to—get—them—out—of—there." He spaced his words for emphasis and looked, Judy thought, very masculine and stern.

"YIP," BARKED THE PUPPIES IN EXCITED
agreement. "Yip, yip, yow!" They were every bit as
anxious to get to Lynn and the twins as the three on
the edge of the quarry hole were to rescue them.

Jeff began to study the situation. On the other side
of the quarry from where he crouched there was a
steep path down. Many a time he'd skidded to the
bottom of the pit just for the fun of clambering up
again. But as he'd just told the girls, climbing the

quarry wall with a wriggling puppy in his arms would be to court suicide. Even if he managed to maintain his own footing there was the danger that he might drop the dog.

"We could lower a rope," Judy suggested, "and tie the dogs on it, one by one."

"And haul them up the side of the cliff," added Lynn.

Jeff shook his head. "They'd be terrified," he said. "Besides, you'd be bound to bang them against the side of the quarry on the way up."

"If we were careful?" Judy asked.

"Even if you were very careful. Remember, they'd be fighting for dear life!"

Judy rocked back on her heels. "O.K., that's out. But there's got to be some way."

"Let me think," urged Jeff. His mind worked slowly and methodically, and he was always annoyed when his twin rushed him into precarious conclusions.

"How would they do it in the movies?" Lynn mused. She didn't feel that the three of them were quite capable of coping with the situation without professional help.

Jeff snapped his fingers. "That's it! A basket. They'd use a basket. I've seen 'em do it dozens of times."

"A basket?" Judy looked dubious.

"Sure. An ordinary market basket—a strong one with a handle. We could tie the pup in."

"Not in any we have down home you couldn't," Judy declared. "They're all wobbly as the dickens."

"How about you, Lynn?" Jeff asked.

Lynn shook her head. "Ours is too small."

"I know!" Judy broke in. "A shopping basket. The kind that's very deep. You push it around on wheels. Mother has a good sturdy one. That would be just the thing!"

At once they were all agreed. Jeff raced off toward home for the basket, and Lynn and Judy hurried back to the Matthews' garage to untangle a stout length of rope. As they left the quarry they could hear the puppies' despairing wails at being deserted.

Judy took time out to call back to them: "Be patient now, dogs! We won't be long!"

Jeff shook his head in mock despair and called over his shoulder, "Of course they'll understand!"

Finally the paraphernalia of rescue was accumulated. When Jeff came up the hill lugging the basket the girls were still busy untangling rope. "I've broken two fingernails already," Judy complained as she pulled impatiently at a knot. "Jeff, you help."

Lynn went off to the house and returned with a piece of clothesline with which to tie the pups into their temporary cage. "Be sure to do it very securely," she cautioned Jeff. "They're squirmers!"

Back at the quarry the pups set up their frantic barking again the minute the trio returned. Jeff circled the top of the wall and started down the steep path while Lynn and Judy lowered the basket down the sheer side of the excavation with the rope.

At the strange sight of the basket approaching through the air Boy and Brother started to bark more furiously than ever. Judy and Lynn began to giggle with excitement. It was the kind of giggling that, once started, was hard to stop. Jeff, skidding and sliding down the shelving stone path, looked deadly serious, and he only increased their mirth. "Wouldn't it be funny," Judy chuckled, "if we had to pull Jeff up too?"

"He'd fit in the basket about up to his knees," Lynn replied, and at the imaginary picture she drew both girls laughed again.

"Hey!" Jeff called from below. "Quit giggling and get to work." He had almost reached the bottom of the stone cup and the dogs were now utterly distracted, not knowing whether to run toward Jeff or to wait and see what manner of thing was descending on them from above.

Jeff settled it. "Here, Boy! Here, Brother!" he called.

As the dogs turned and ran across the slippery rock formation to obey his command Judy suddenly stopped laughing. She looked more closely at the dog nearest her—Brother. She always knew him from Boy, even at a distance, by the set of his ears. It seemed, as she watched him, that he limped a little. "Look, Lynn," she started to say. But at that moment Jeff called to them to throw down the clothesline, and when she looked again she thought she must have been mistaken. He was greeting Jeff with as much enthusiasm as Boy.

It took some time for their exuberance to calm, and Jeff very sensibly waited. He sat down and let them lick his face and bite his hands affectionately, talking to them softly in a voice intended to soothe their nerves. Finally it seemed to him that it would be safe to risk the first ascent.

"Come on, Boy," he said. "You're going for an elevator ride." He stroked the dog gently and talked to him in a composed, quiet tone as he slid him into the basket. Still talking, he crisscrossed the clothesline again and again through the slats at the top, darning the rope in and out to make a strong shield against any sudden leap. "All right," he said finally. "Ready? And no matter what you do, don't let go!"

Lynn stood back from the rock wall and hitched the rope around the trunk of a small tree. Judy braced her feet against a root and together they started to pull. It was slow work. From the bottom of the quarry Jeff had to guide them, shouting directions, lest the rope or the basket catch on a jagged edge of rock. Again and again they had to lower it a few feet, and take a new position. All the time the puppy inside the basket was wailing in uninhibited fright.

Finally, however, Judy called: "All right! I've got him!" and pulled the basket the last few inches to firm ground by its handle. With fingers aching from the exertion of the long tug she helped Lynn to loosen the restraining clothesline. Still trembling, but ecstatic with relief, Boy wriggled through, and while Judy held him in her arms Lynn lowered the basket back down the rock wall to collect his brother.

When Jeff lowered the remaining pup into the wicker basket the dog cried piteously, almost as though he were in pain. Lynn shook her head. "Nervous as hoot owls," she said. "They always have been. As different from Shadow and Sambo as day is from night."

Judy couldn't help agreeing with her. Now that she was more familiar with cocker spaniels as a breed, these two pups even looked different to her. They were a little sway-backed, for one thing, their legs seeming too short for their bodies. And their coats lacked the magnificent sheen . . .

"Watch it!" Jeff interrupted her thought. "Easy! Move a little to the right."

Judy moved, wishing that just for a moment she could bend her aching arms at the elbow. The taut rope seemed to catch.

"Whoa!" Jeff called.

"What's the matter?" Judy couldn't see over the edge of the cliff.

"You struck a snag. Try moving back to the left."

Again Judy followed Jeff's directions, but the rope remained caught.

"Try lowering it a little."

Judy let the rope out cautiously and felt it go slack. "Nope!" Jeff yelled. "The basket's caught."

Judy edged forward and peered down. Halfway up the side of the quarry the basket spun on a two-foot length of rope from a jagged cut in a rock which protruded from the wall. Inside, the caged puppy yelped in terror, throwing his weight against his wicker prison but as unable as was Judy to dislodge the rope from the crevice. The drop from where Judy lay, flat on her stomach, was sheer. The ascent from where Jeff stood frowning up at her only a bird could have conquered. Between them, more frantic with every passing moment, dangled Brother.

To both the twins, the danger was immediately obvious. Fighting his confinement, Brother was sawing the rope against the sharp edge of the rock. It would be only a matter of time before the hemp would ravel and break, dropping the puppy to certain destruction on the quarry floor.

Judy's heart leaped to her throat. "What can I do?" she called down to Jeff frantically. "He's cutting the rope!"

Jeff, as well as his sister, felt helpless. "Whatever you do, hang onto that line!" she shouted back. "He just may work himself loose."

But neither of the twins really believed that the pup would be his own salvation. The rope was far too securely caught.

Behind her Judy could hear Lynn's voice, surprisingly calm. "Can you take the full weight of the rope if I let go?"

"I—I think so. Wait till I get braced."

"All right?"

"All right." Judy couldn't imagine what Lynn planned to do, but anyone with a course of action was needed desperately at that moment. She pushed with both feet against the stanch roots of an oak and waited.

Lynn was moving about somewhere behind her. It seemed risky even to turn her head to discover what she was doing. Any moment the slack rope might become taut. The weight would increase with a sudden snap. Judy would have to be ready.

She made herself believe that this was what would happen. The alternative was too dreadful to contemplate. She shut her eyes and swallowed hard. Her throat felt swollen and dry.

"Hurry!" she managed to say. "Hurry, Lynn."

Lynn was moving toward the edge of the cliff as she spoke, coming around to Judy's right. She was carrying a long, thin branch of a dogwood, ripping shorter branches from it as she came.

At once Judy realized what she intended to do. "If only it's long enough!" she prayed.

Lynn knelt at the edge of the quarry, then wriggled forward and lay flat, entwining both feet around a short stump. Carefully she worked the long branch forward in her hands until she was grasping it close to the thick end.

"Be careful!" Jeff cried from below.

Lynn didn't waste breath to answer him. "Steady, Judy!" she panted. "I think I can make it. Can you handle the weight?"

Judy wound the rope twice around the palm of her hand, cutting into the flesh. She wasn't at all sure she could handle it, but she shouted, "Go ahead." She knew now what Lynn was trying to do. If she could work the branch under the rope and lift it up and out so that it would again swing free Brother could be saved.

The next few seconds passed with agonizing slowness. Judy was aware at once that Lynn's position on the very edge of the quarry wall was nearly as precarious as the dog's, that the weight of the branch in her slender hands must be almost past endurance, and that the effort to dislodge the rope might hasten, rather than forestall, its breaking. But she knew at the same time that they had to take the chance. Lynn was acting with coolheaded common sense. If Brother could be hauled to safety he'd owe his life to her.

Nobody spoke, but the echoing yelps of the captive dog formed a background of frenzied sound. Lynn strained downward, breathing hard. Then, simultaneously, Jeff yelled and the rope tautened, knocking Judy forward to her knees.

"Lynn! Help!" she gasped. For a desperate moment it seemed as though she couldn't hold on. Then Lynn was beside her, taking part of the weight, and in another ten seconds the two girls had the basket itself in their hands.

Jeff scrambled up the ragged stone path as fast as he could come. When he reached Lynn he was vociferous in his praise. "Boy, I'll sure hand it to you! Not another girl I know would have risked it!" Together they all examined the fraying rope. "Three more minutes and he'd have been a goner!" Jeff declared.

The trio walked back to the Matthews' rather quietly, weary with tension. Boy and Brother, whistled in by Lynn, stayed close at heel. Judy's eyes followed the dogs curiously. They looked none the worse for their week away from home. Their coats were not matted or filled with burrs. Wherever they had been they'd received good treatment. Of that she was sure. If only dogs could talk—could answer a few questions. In a way she couldn't justify Judy kept feeling that their disappearance and their strange return had some bearing on the mystery that was still paramount in her mind.

It was nearly noon when the twins reached home. Jeff ate an enormous lunch while Judy, still too excited to be exclusively interested in food, described the thrilling rescue of the puppies to her mother and Mamam. Neither of them could hazard a guess as to how the dogs happened to end their week's journey in the quarry hole, but Mamam made an acute observation. "Lynn goes up a good bit in my estimation," she said, "if she'd do all that for a puppy she doesn't even claim to own."

Bringing up that angle of the situation led Jeff to ask a question. "Did you call Mr. Gross?"

Mamam nodded brightly, glad for the chance to spring her surprise. "I did," she said. "Young Art certainly sounded surprised when I said I'd be glad to have the puppy."

Judy clapped her hands. "O Mamam, what fun!" she cried. "When's he coming?"

Mamam raised both eyebrows and grinned benignly. "This very afternoon."

The wait for the Gross Point station wagon seemed endless for Judy. But finally it turned into the drive and the kennelman, now familiar to all of them, lifted King Cole's duplicate from the box in the back. When he delivered the dog's leash into Mamam's gnarled hands the man seemed puzzled. "That's a very fine dog you have there," he kept repeating. "A very fine dog!"

The twins could scarcely contain themselves until the fellow's departure. Even before the station wagon gathered speed they dropped to the grass and ran impatient fingers up the dog's front legs.

"Lynn was right!" Judy cried. "He hasn't any dewclaws!"

Jeff, more deliberate in his investigation, nodded. He told Mamam, "You can feel them plain as anything on Boy and Brother."

Mamam, now that she was the spaniel's owner, looked down on him in considerable dismay. "Well, I hope that'll mean Mr. Matthews can prove ownership," she said, "for what I'd ever do with this puppy in Camden I don't rightly know."

The twins were of course agog with impatience to take the pup up to see Lynn. Neither of them could find a fault that would make the dog undesirable for showing and thus explain the strange nature of the gift, but they felt that Lynn's opinion would be more expert than their own.

"Go ahead," Mamam urged them. "Take him out of my sight. Then he won't keep reminding me what an addlebrained old woman I am to allow myself to be talked into such a proposition as becoming a dog owner at my age."

"Oh, you don't really mean that!" Judy protested, hugging the puppy. "He's *beautiful!*"

"Of course he's beautiful!" Mamam agreed. "But so are the pair of Staffordshire spaniels I have home on my mantelpiece. And they don't have to be fed three times a day!"

Lynn was standing on the porch of the Matthews' house when the twins reached the top of the hill. Boy and Brother were with her, feeding out of a low pan.

"Oo-hoo! Lynn!" Judy called, and Lynn turned. The minute she saw the twins' companion she raced down the lawn and through the sagging gate to fall on her knees and gather the black dog into her arms.

"Sambo!" she cried. "My baby! Are you all right?"

Jeff, uncomfortable under the stress of what he called "female dramatics," said: "He looks all right to me. That's what we brought him up to find out."

Lynn sat back and examined the dog minutely, running her hands down his back and flanks, examining his ears and mouth. "He's handsomer than ever," she exclaimed, "and in the pink of condition."

"How do you know it's Sambo and not Shadow?" Judy broke in. "They look exactly alike to us."

Lynn glanced up innocently. "I just know, that's all. You are Sambo, aren't you?" she asked, emphasizing the name, and the dog wagged his tail in reply.

Just then Boy and Brother, having finished their food, frisked up to the group. They were anxious to inspect this canine newcomer, and they sniffed and danced around him, barking. Judy laughed at their antics. They were nice pups. But even novices like Judy and Jeff could see that they no more measured up to Sambo than a neon sign does to the evening star.

"About the dewclaws," Jeff cut in. "You were right, Lynn. D'you suppose now your dad will be able to prove . . . ?"

But a short cry from his sister interrupted him. Boy had crept onto her lap and she was fondling him, running her hands down his legs. "Look!" Judy said importunately, "Boy's dewclaws are gone!"

JUDY'S CRY LED
to an examination from
which a strange certainty
emerged. Neither Boy nor Brother any longer possessed
the dewclaws with which they had been born. The one
possibility that Lynn might be able to prove her ownership of Shadow and Sambo had vanished into thin air.

Lynn, oddly, seemed less perturbed by the discovery
than the twins. "It would have been hard to make
a case of it, anyway. There was only Dad's word and
mine—and we're poor people." She shrugged cyni-
cally.

Judy stamped her foot. "Lynn Matthews, stop talking like that!" she commanded. "You ought to be
ashamed. This is a democratic country and if Shadow
and Sambo really belong to you there isn't any reason
in the world why you shouldn't fight for them. Haven't
you got any courage?"

The outburst surprised both Lynn and Jeff, but
Lynn's eyes remained sullen. "Money and prestige are
hard things to fight," she said.

As they walked home later Judy still boiled with

rage. "Lynn's too meek," she told Jeff accusingly. "She ought to be more scrappy."

"Like you."

"All right. Like me!" Judy kicked a stone ahead of her with the toe of her shoe.

Jeff couldn't hide a smile. "Look out. You'll get hurt," he said mildly.

Judy took another interpretation from the remark. "So what?" she asked with slangy belligerence. "I'd rather get into a peck of trouble than I would sit around doing nothing and worrying about being the underdog. That's why people *are* underdogs—because they haven't enough spirit to get to be top dogs!"

"Dogs, dogs, dogs. That's all we seem to talk about." Jeff, still grinning, heaved a manufactured sigh.

Judy whirled on her twin. "You're as bad as Lynn. We've got to *do* something!"

"All right," agreed Jeff. "You do it! I think we've reached an impasse myself. We have a dozen overripe suspicions and we can't prove one of them. Especially not without Lynn's help."

"Are you backing down too?" Judy's lip curled.

"I'm just being sensible," Jeff retorted.

"Sensible? I think you're just stalling." Judy spread her slender arms, Joan of Arc fashion. "This is a time for action!" she cried.

Jeff was fed up with heroics. "Well, go ahead—act!" he snapped back.

Judy's arms dropped to her sides. Her voice became

deceptively calm. "Very well," she said, looking her brother direct in the eyes. "I will."

Jeff didn't say a word but his whole expression taunted his twin: You're bluffing, Judy, and you know it! He could have spoken the words aloud, they were so clear.

The girl's eyes dropped before her brother's. She *was* bluffing, but at the same time she felt convinced that if she'd only follow each road to its logical conclusion she'd find some way out of this maze.

It was hard for Judy to sit down and think things through. She operated on hunches, leaped to conclusions. Jeff was the brain of the pair, and now she felt that he had deserted. For once in her life she was going to have to move forward on her own.

A dozen times during the evening she regretted her bravado, but each time she could see her twin's challenging eyes as he'd faced her: All right, Judy, *do* something—if you can!

She went to bed early and shut the door between her room and the connecting bath. But she didn't go to sleep. She sat with her arms clasped around her hunched knees and once more retraced all the paths she and Jeff had followed in trying to track down the culprit in the mystery of the black spaniels.

Until Mr. Gross had given Mamam the dog Judy had picked him for the thief. But, she reasoned, he'd scarcely give away something he'd been to so much trouble to steal. Not, anyway, without some very strong reason. And, search as she would, Judy could find no reason for giving Mamam a thousand-dollar present.

Two puppies. Two thousand dollars. Fantastically valuable dogs in Judy's eyes. But would two thousand dollars loom large to Artemus Gross? She thought not. He could have bought the puppies, not stolen them, unless . . .

Judy's small hands, cold in spite of the warmth of the summer night, clenched more tightly. Unless the owner of the pups wouldn't sell! But then why give them away to the Matthews? For it was obvious that the Matthews couldn't afford to buy such dogs. And why, in turn, would Mr. Gross present a puppy to Mamam? It didn't make sense.

It was at this point that Judy's mind always stopped. Parts of the puzzle fitted together logically enough. Then, when she tried to fit other parts, the whole picture disintegrated.

It was the unreasonableness of Mr. Gross's conduct that had stopped Jeff, and that was stopping her.

Oh, bother, Judy thought. Let it be unreasonable. Skip it. Concentrate on something else. There's no use going around and around on the same line like a broken phonograph record. It's getting me nowhere fast.

The moon, shining full through the casement window, rose higher and higher in the sky. Judy shifted position and lay with her chin in her hands, ruefully

biting a corner of her lower lip. With more patience than she'd ever exercised in her life before, she rehearsed every step of the way they had traveled, from the moment they had first seen Shadow and Sambo to the happenings of this very day. She was looking for something she'd skipped, for some clue that perhaps, at the time, hadn't seemed to be a clue. That was the way, in books, mysteries were always worked out.

Nothing! At least, nothing new.

All right, Judy promised herself, I'll begin again. She rolled over on her back and stared up at the placid moon. We were sitting down by the road, waiting for the postman . . .

Judy could see the scene. Every detail of it was etched forever on her brain. Suddenly she gave a little gasp and sat up abruptly. She snapped her fingers. "That's it!" she whispered aloud. "Of course!"

She almost jumped out of bed, to go in and wake Jeff. Then she thought better of it. "Go ahead—act!" he'd said, jeering. Very well, she would.

For ten more minutes she sat quite still, her forehead on her knees, her loosened hair falling forward, trying to think what the best way would be. Then she slipped down to the floor and crept down the back stairs in her bare feet. Moonlight flooded the silent house and made it easy to go to the desk in the study, to find note paper and fountain pen. Noiselessly she hurried back to her room.

In the morning she was up before Jeff and ate breakfast with her father. Immediately afterward, with the third draft of a painstakingly written letter tucked in the pocket of her play suit, she wheeled her bicycle out of the garage and pedaled off toward Wayne.

Once the stamp was attached and the envelope was pushed into the post-office slot Judy was in an agony of apprehension. Suppose she was wrong? Suppose the letter never reached its destination? Suppose she waited and waited, then never knew!

On the way home the other alternatives began to assail her. Suppose everybody was very angry? Suppose she'd acted like a fool, playing a hunch as crazy as this.

But it wasn't crazy! Judy's self-esteem leaped to her aid. It wasn't silly. It was smart. It was the only possible way the whole thing could be worked out.

To keep the secret from Jeff and Mamam was a high ordeal. Judy could only manage it by avoiding them both as much as possible. She begged her mother for household chores that would keep her occupied. Then, with a dust mop in her hands, she would sit for hours and dream. "Don't you feel well, Judy?" Mrs. Sutherland asked one day when she found her daughter in a trance in the living room. She placed an apprehensive hand on Judy's forehead. Such a surge of domestic ambition combined with these odd lapses seemed very alarming indeed.

Mamam and Jeff moped. They were both entirely aware that they'd lost the most vital member of their team. Mamam was at a loss to account for Judy's change of heart, but Jeff knew that his sister had taken his rather caustic challenge as ridicule. As the week wore on he made blundering overtures, trying to get back on a normal friendly footing, but Judy continued to shy away. She didn't trust her self-control in Jeff's presence—yet if she told him, then found that she was wrong . . .

Thursday and Friday dragged by, bland summer days that passed with uneventful pace. By Saturday morning Judy was counting on her fingers and feeling as nervous as a skittish colt.

The week end was insufferably hot. Even Sambo lay panting in the shade of the terrace awning, disregarding Jeff's languid invitation to play. Mamam, feeling the heat less than any of them, crocheted on and on. Mr. Sutherland patched the screen door and Mrs. Sutherland weeded the chrysanthemum beds where the shade of the pine trees reached them. Judy, her nervous anticipation spent, was sunk in a mood of black depression. She lay on the flagstones with a book in front of her, neither reading nor thinking, just marking mental time.

It was on Sunday evening at seven o'clock that the telephone rang.

Judy started up, then sank back. Jeff answered it. The family could hear the adolescent break of his voice as he said, "Hello." A minute later he walked back to the terrace. "It's for you, Judy," he said, his eyes faintly puzzled.

"For me?" Judy's heart leaped to her throat. "One of the girls?" she added, trying to quench her rising hopes. But even before Jeff shook his head she knew!

It was all Jeff could do to resist following his twin back into the house, so sharply was his curiosity aroused. But that would be kid stuff—beneath him. Deliberately he sat down in a deck chair and stretched his long legs out and crossed them, ears straining to catch some hint of the conversation going on inside. There was Judy's weak "Hello," then a breathless, "Yes—yes, I did," but Mr. Sutherland, turning the pages of the Sunday paper started to read an item aloud to his wife, and Jeff fretted with impatience, not able to hear another word.

In a minute there was the click of the receiver on the hook, but Judy didn't come out of the house at once. Mr. Sutherland folded his paper and dropped it to the terrace. His wife stretched languidly and said, "Let's wander up to the Rogers', George," and together they strolled away. Jeff watched them go, arm in arm, stopping here and there to examine a shrub or a bed of perennials. Finally he turned to Mamam. "Judy's up to something, and I don't know what," he said.

Mamam, who had been unsuspicious, looked up from her crocheting. "Judy?" At the same moment the subject of their conversation appeared in the doorway.

If she had wanted to time an entrance, she could have managed it no better. Both Jeff and Mamam looked toward her at once, and as she opened the screen door and stepped out to the terrace she had their undivided attention.

"Miss Amelia Carstairs," she said, "is on her way out here to see me."

Mamam's eyebrows raised, but she didn't lose a stitch. Jeff repeated the name incredulously. "Miss Amelia Carstairs?" he said. "I thought she had moved out West."

Judy nodded. "She had. She's just come back."

The trip out from Wayne to the Sutherlands' took only eight minutes by car. Before any other conversation was possible there was the sound of rubber tires on the drive. Suddenly Judy turned to Mamam, beseeching. "You'd better come with us," she said. "I'm scared."

Jeff heard the word "us" in considerable relief. Whatever Judy was cooking up, he wanted to be in on the party.

The knocker clacked sharply on the front door and

Judy walked slowly to answer it. "Better bring her out here," Mamam said. "It's too hot to sit in the living room."

Afterward, Judy couldn't remember how she reached the door. She never knew that her movement toward it was deliberate. She would have guessed that she ran. Now, at this final moment, a thousand doubts pressed down upon her. Suppose her meddling were to hurt Lynn and her father, rather than help them! Suppose . . .

The woman who stood silhouetted against the setting sun was tall and slender. Although her face was in shadow she seemed younger than Judy had anticipated. A straw sailor was perched firmly on a mass of gray hair, and in spite of the humidity of the day the print traveling suit she wore looked crisp and unmussed.

"Good evening," she said at once, in a voice that was husky and abrupt. "I'm Amelia Carstairs, of course."

"W-won't you come in?" Judy stepped back to let her pass. "If you'll go right through the hall to the terrace. It's cooler out there."

Miss Carstairs nodded. She swept past Judy on sensible Cuban heels, and her skirts, longer than the fashion, rustled slightly as she walked. If it weren't for her shoes, Judy thought briefly, she'd make an elegant ghost. She could almost see her tall, willowy form stalking the corridors of Carstairs' Castle, dressed in the Gibson girl clothes of that ancient photograph . . .

But there was nothing ghostly about Miss Carstairs' manner. She still retained the command that had made her a powerful personality in her day and had also kept her a spinster. At the screen door she paused, head erect. Judy pushed it open and followed her to the terrace. Weakly, she made the introductions.

"Miss Carstairs, Mrs. Whiteman and my brother Jeff."

"Good evening." Miss Carstairs nodded briskly, but her eyes were on the black cocker wriggling from under Mamam's chair. Unexpectedly, the lady whistled. "Here, boy!"

Sambo advanced at once, pink tongue lolling from the heat, but head high and tail wagging.

The visitor dropped her handbag on the nearest chair. She leaned down and cradled the pup's chin in one hand while she ran the other along his short, straight back. A smile touched her thin lips briefly. "He's more magnificent than I dared hope!" she murmured as though she were talking to herself.

Judy shifted restlessly from one foot to another. "But—can you tell?—is he *yours?*"

MISS CARSTAIRS ROSE, ONE HAND HOLD-
ing Sambo's forefeet, the other supporting his body.
"Child," she said, smiling down at Judy, "if a dog
ever stood as the epitome of a breeding tradition, this
dog does. He's Carstairs through and through."

Judy sighed profoundly. "I was sure of it!" she
cried. "Oh, I was certain! Especially after I remembered the Delaware, Ohio, postmark on that letter.
It just couldn't have come from anyone but you!"

"It could." Miss Carstairs' smile widened to a grin.
"There are several thousand people in Delaware. But
as it happened, it didn't. You were an extremely ob-
serving girl."

"What's this all about?" Jeff cut in, still puzzled.
"Did you write Miss Carstairs in Ohio, Judy?"

Judy nodded happily. "Delaware," she said dreamily. "Don't you remember the letter in the Matthews'
postbox the day we found the pups? It was such a
funny name, it always stuck in my mind. Then later
Mr. Jones, down at the drugstore, said Miss Amelia

had moved West. Oh, I was stupid not to think of it sooner!"

Mamam jabbed her needle into her crocheting and spoke for the first time, and with considerable asperity. "Now look here," she said, "you may as well stop talking in riddles, Judith. It isn't polite. You and Miss Carstairs may know what this is all about, but Jeffrey and I do not. Suppose you start at the beginning."

It was Miss Carstairs, not Judy, who answered. She settled herself in a canvas chair, Sambo still on her lap. "The beginning," she said, "was a good many years ago. Maybe I'd better start the story myself."

Judy nodded and sat down, cross-legged, on the flagstones.

"It was when father was still alive, and the Carstairs fortunes were more or less intact. I made a hobby of breeding cocker spaniels." The lady glanced down and stroked Sambo's silky coat. "My kennels were never large, but I had a few fine dogs. Gay Lady was one of them. But I had an idea that by careful line breeding and persistent culling I could breed even better cockers than the Gay Lady strain. I mapped out a pretty extensive plan when, quite unexpectedly, my father died, and it became apparent that there wasn't much left in the way of worldly wealth except the house.

"I may as well tell you that even that was mortgaged, very heavily indeed. I simplified my living, cut off most of the rooms, let all but a few of the dogs go, and became, I suppose, something of a recluse."

Miss Carstairs' mouth twisted wryly at the corners. "I suppose," she went on, glancing from Judy to Jeff, "that you youngsters would say that I wasn't trained to face reality. Very few of my class and generation were. It never occurred to me to let the house go, move to simpler quarters, and go into spaniel-breeding as a business. I simply disrupted my life as little as possible and went right on breeding dogs. For pleasure, mind you, not for profit. Those I had to sell went into private families as pets.

"Well, the inevitable happened," said Miss Carstairs with a shrug. "Embarrassing bills began to pile up. I had to let my last servant—the gardener—go, and make out with Matthews coming in one day a week. I liked Matthews. He was honest and conscientious, if a little mealy-mouthed, and he took a great interest in the dogs. He knew about my breeding plan and had confidence in it. As a matter of fact he was with me on the morning this pup was born." She paused for a moment, and, raising the dog's head, looked into the gentle black eyes.

"I'm sure that by now you will have guessed," she said, "that Shadow and Sambo are the acme of what I had been striving for in cocker perfection. Even as babies I was sure they'd live up to my expectations. They were strong and handsome and close coupled and even then their heads were promising. Mike Matthews was almost as enthusiastic as I.

"Then one morning Artemus Gross came to the house and wanted to look at the pups. Of course I showed them to him. As another breeder I thought his interest was purely professional. But when he offered to buy them I refused."

Miss Carstairs paused again. "Mr. Gross," she said more slowly, "is a man who won't take no for an answer. First he raised his price. I shook my head. 'These dogs are not for sale,' I explained. Then he had the temerity to call my financial position to my attention. I ordered him out of the house. Three days later I discovered for the first time who held father's mortgage on the property. Artemus Gross foreclosed. Before he took this step, however, he telephoned me and tried to bribe me. 'Let me have those two black pups,' he said, 'and you can stay on in your house as long as you live.' To a Carstairs, he said that!"

Mamam sniffed explosively. "Sounds like one of Old Art's tricks," she muttered, but Miss Amelia might not have heard her, so engrossed was she in her own tale.

"Gross held a chattel mortgage too. He started moving paintings and furniture out of the house even before I left. Maybe he thought I'd weaken even then. He's not much of a judge of character."

Judy was remembering the Victorian chairs that Mamam had described as gracing the Gross Point dining room. It must have been heartbreaking for Miss Amelia to see her heirlooms go. Mr. Gross was even more cold-blooded than she would have believed.

"I finally left Wayne," Miss Carstairs was continuing, "to go to my sister in Ohio, owing quite a few small bills. Perhaps, from the point of view of my creditors I should have sold Shadow and Sambo at once. Yet I kept feeling that if I could raise one or both of the puppies they would repay me a thousand-fold and allow me to clear my obligations entirely. The temptation was too great. I gave the puppies to Mike Matthews and his daughter to raise, with the enjoinder to let no one—absolutely no one—know they came from me. Gross is a persuasive as well as a powerful man. I didn't trust him.

"I might say here that Matthews never knew that Artemus Gross and I had any argument over the dogs. It was a personal matter, one that it could not benefit me to discuss."

Here Jeff blurted out, "Did you know Mr. Gross had fired Matthews?"

"He didn't fire him. Mr. Matthews left!" corrected Judy loyally.

"I never even knew Mike had worked at Gross Point," said Miss Carstairs. "He was always very reticent on the subject of his previous job. But I trusted Matthews implicitly. He was kindly, and he knew dogs. It was the most natural thing in the world that I should leave the puppies in his care. The only thing I can't understand is why, when Shadow and Sambo were stolen, he wouldn't have got in touch with me at once."

"But don't you see?" Judy exclaimed. "He was frightened. Lynn and her father are just alike. They're honest and sweet and all that, but they won't stand up and scrap. Circumstances can whip them as fast as I can snap my fingers."

Jeff nodded. "I've worked with Mr. Matthews," he said. "Judy's right. D'you know how I'll bet he figured? He knew Gross had stolen the dogs, but he didn't know how. And after he came down and talked to Dad that night he realized that Gross's neat trick of unloading the substitute puppies had queered any case he might have had."

"Then Mr. Gross did substitute the puppies?" Judy broke in.

"Sure, that's obvious now." Jeff explained to Miss Carstairs just how the ruse could have been worked. Mr. Gross must have known that both father and daughter expected to be away from the Matthews place for the day. The exchange would have been easy to make. The only thing he hadn't counted on was the carelessness of the kennelman who, not knowing the value of these new puppies, left the pen door unlocked.

"And of course that explains," Judy broke in excitedly, "why the pups weren't heading either to Gross Point or up the lane to the Matthews' when we found them."

"Why?" Jeff was a little slow.

"Because they were going home—to Carstairs' Castle, of course!"

Mamam clicked her teeth dubiously. "Those little pups?"

Miss Carstairs nodded, agreeing with Judy. "It's perfectly plausible," she said. "They'd been with the Matthews only about two weeks. Once on the loose, they'd turn toward the place they'd been raised. Of course they were young to show so much sense, but intelligence is bred into a fine dog."

Mamam accepted this explanation for what it was worth. "Then I'm to understand," she added, "that when Young Art—that's Mr. Gross—couldn't buy the dogs from you, he was determined to get them by hook or by crook, so he stole them?"

"And apparently substituted two black puppies of about the same age from his own kennel," Miss Carstairs agreed.

"Well, I'll be!" mused Mamam. "But I'm not surprised, not surprised a bit. I could tell you stories about Old Art Gross . . ."

Jeff forestalled such an eventuality. "Have you talked with Mr. Matthews?" he asked Miss Amelia.

"No. Not yet." Judy saw the vertical lines in the visitor's forehead deepen, the dark eyes grow perplexed. She could tell it was an ordeal to which Miss Amelia did not look forward.

Impulsively the girl leaned forward. "Don't blame Mr. Matthews too much!" she urged. "You know how worried he must have been, all these weeks, with the wrong dogs in his kennel, and the thought of facing you." She tried to put herself in the gardener's place, share his point of view. "He must be very scared of Mr. Gross. Remember, Mr. Gross tried to ruin him once before, and almost succeeded. Mr. Matthews knew nobody'd believe his story—nobody, that is, except maybe Jeff and me. And we're just kids."

"What about me?" bridled Mamam. "I suppose I'm just an old lady in my dotage, and I don't count."

"You *do* count!" Judy corrected her. "She's been wonderful, Miss Carstairs. Just wonderful!"

"Stop passing bouquets and let's go on with the unraveling," suggested Jeff with a grin. "You'll have to agree, Miss Carstairs, that Mike Matthews found himself in a spot. He hated to admit to you that he'd lost your prize dogs, and he was probably clinging to some vague hope that he could get them back before you discovered anything. He had one ace up his sleeve, you know."

"What?" Miss Carstairs asked.

"He knew you could identify your pups by the missing dewclaws."

"Exactly. That's all the more reason why he should have let me know at once."

"I don't know," Jeff replied. "Maybe he thought Gross would be unscrupulous enough to brazen the thing out and let you both fight him. Maybe he thought such a claim would never hold in court. Or maybe he was sacrificing the obligation he had to you for Lynn's sake."

"I don't quite understand," said Miss Carstairs.

"What I'm trying to say is that Mike might simply have been afraid to lose the days' work he's got together. It wouldn't take Mr. Gross very long to spread a few unsavory stories . . ."

For the first time sympathy softened Miss Carstairs' eyes. "I suppose you're right, young man," she said. "I'll try not to be too hard on him."

Bringing up the matter of the dewclaws led Judy to tell of the strange disappearance and return of the substitute cockers, Boy and Brother. "Of course now," she said, "I'm sure it was Mr. Gross's doing. Somehow he must have learned that the missing fifth toes would be our only way of identifying the right pups. But how?"

Jeff looked thoughtful. He turned to Mamam. "Remember the day you called at Gross Point?"

Mamam nodded.

"Mr. Gross was out, wasn't he, when you arrived?"

"Yes, he was."

"Did he say where?"

For her age, Mamam's memory was exceptional. "He'd been down to the veterinary's," she said at once.

Jeff nodded, and pounded his head with his fists. "I'm an idiot!" he scolded himself. "A dyed-in-the-wool nincompoop. That one just lay around staring me in the face and I missed it cold."

"Missed what?" Judy was getting impatient.

"That was the afternoon," Jeff explained to his twin, "when Dr. Clark and I had that long conversation about dewclaws. It's a cinch Gross was in his office at the time. Can't you just see him, after the doctor hung up, saying: 'Who was that you were talking to? Sounded like a youngster.' The doc wouldn't have thought anything of it. He'd have said, 'George Sutherland's boy,' quick as a flash."

Judy clapped her hands. "Of course! Then Mr. Gross had to cover his one error and get Boy and Brother back, so he could have their dewclaws removed too."

A trace of a smile crossed Miss Carstairs' face, but to the twins it went unnoticed. Jeff's eyes suddenly widened, as a disagreeable thought struck him. "Suppose Mr. Gross sticks to his story—that Shadow and Sambo are his. How could you ever disprove it, Miss Carstairs, with the evidence of the dewclaws destroyed?"

Miss Carstairs' smile broadened. "I think I can handle Mr. Gross," she said.

"Will you call the police?" Judy asked hopefully.

The visitor shook her head. "I don't think that will be necessary. I had been planning simply to call on Mr. Gross with a couple of friends of mine, but now it occurs to me that it might be more interesting to invite him down here."

"But would he come?" Judy's eyes sparkled with

anticipation, but at the same time she was dubious. The master of Gross Point was suspicious. He might suspect a ruse.

"I think he would, if Mrs. Whiteman suggested it. After all, he has a special interest in you now," Miss Carstairs said, turning to the elderly lady. "As Sambo's nominal owner . . ."

"That's one thing I still can't understand—why he'd ever give away Sambo." Jeff shook his head.

"To put it colloquially," replied Miss Amelia with a smile, "you had him on the run, Jeff. I think Artemus Gross figured that a dog in the hand is worth two in the Matthews kennels, and that to give away a valuable puppy to one of the group that had him under surveillance would be to throw you all completely off the scent."

"That's right!" Mamam piped up. "I always did say Young Art was smart. I'll bet that's just what he thought."

"I'll admit that move had me buffaloed," Jeff said.

"But now let's get down to business. How can we persuade Mr. Gross to call—at some particular hour, say, tomorrow evening?" Miss Carstairs looked at Mamam, and Mamam was ready for her.

"That's easy," she said at once. "I'll arrange that. I'll simply tell Young Art I'm afraid the pup is going to be too much for me, that I'd like to give him back, but that I want to talk to him personally when I do." She chuckled to herself. "He'll come a-running!"

IT WAS A CURIOUS JURY THAT GATHERED
at the Sutherland house the next evening. In the living
room were Miss Carstairs, Mamam, Dr. Clark, the
vet, and a stranger whom Miss Carstairs introduced as
"my friend Mr. Ingersoll." In the study were Lynn
and her father with Boy. Brother had been left at
home. The twins darted from one group to the other,
but their parents kept discreetly out of the way. Although apprised, now, of the entire complicated story,
Mr. and Mrs. Sutherland felt, quite rightly, that this
was Jeff's and Judy's show. In the competent hands of
Miss Carstairs and Mamam, they felt the children
were safe.

Inside the house, the air was still and sullen. Outside, the sky was yellow. For the first time in six weeks
the newspapers prophesied an honest-to-goodness rain.
The early dusk was heavy, threatening. Branches of
the trees near the garage whipped and creaked. It was
a perfect night to apprehend a wrongdoer, and Judy

shivered in excited anticipation as the long Gross car pulled quietly into the drive.

But when she actually opened the front door to Mr. Gross her righteous indignation, which had been mounting steadily since last evening, faded away. She felt almost sorry for this bumptious, unscrupulous fat man whose passion for aggrandizement had led him to forsake the dignity and honor, which, until now, Judy had associated with all grownups.

"Well, young lady, is Mrs. Whiteman in?"

"In the living room, Mr. Gross," Judy replied weakly, knowing the full surprise that would greet him.

But as she preceded him into the long room, where the oddly assorted group of people stood chatting by the fireplace, she had to admit that the master of Gross Point was a cool customer, and her heart hardened again. The man neither hesitated nor changed expression. His wispy eyebrows may have raised a little, and the mottling freckles over his thick nose seemed especially evident, but his voice was level when he said: "What have we here? A tea party?"

Miss Carstairs, her rather long neck held high, broke away from the group. "A reception committee, rather. Good evening, Mr. Gross."

Both Judy and Jeff could readily see, in the conversation that followed, that Miss Amelia was mistress of the situation. She wasted no time on preliminaries and explained that her friends had come together to straighten out a matter of what she felt sure was the mistaken identification of two sets of black spaniel puppies. She gave Mr. Gross a chance to retract his claim gracefully and apologize for being in error, but the kennel owner, as they all suspected, was determined to play the game through.

"I'm afraid these children have been telling you tales that have destroyed your sense of judgment," he said. "King Cole and his brother are obviously Gross Point dogs. The police can substantiate that. Sergeant Cudahy himself saw the papers."

"May I see them?" asked Miss Amelia.

Mr. Gross coughed. "But, my dear lady, of course, any time, any time. Though of course I don't carry them about, nor even leave them at the house. They're in my safe-deposit box in Philadelphia."

"I happen to have my papers here," said Miss Carstairs. "With your permission I should like Mr. Ingersoll to give us his professional judgment on two of the disputed puppies. Mr. Ingersoll," she explained to Mamam and the twins, "is one of the directors of the Schuylkill Valley Kennel Club delegated to give opinions on such matters. He knows the Carstairs' bloodlines well, since both the sire and dam of my two dogs received their championships on his bench. I think, Mr. Gross, he is also familiar with your kennels?"

Mr. Gross had to nod. He had to sit, while Boy and Sambo were brought in, and watch Mr. Ingersoll consider the points of the two dogs. That there was no real comparison everyone in the room knew. Sambo was a show dog and Boy was just a gangly cocker pup, pleasant and appealing, but utterly ordinary. Mr. Ingersoll pointed this out, while Lynn and Mr. Matthews came timidly to the doorway to listen. On the pedigree chart handed to him by Miss Carstairs the judge traced the bloodlines, which, he said decisively, could have terminated successfully in such a dog as Sambo but could scarcely have produced the slight sway-back, the high-set ears, and the brownish eyes which, in his mind, disfigured Boy.

"Nonsense," said Mr. Gross when he had finished. "There are sports in the best of breeding. We all know that."

"Granted," replied Mr. Ingersoll, "but certain characteristics are inherent in a line, and often in an entire kennel. For instance, Mr. Gross, I believe I can recall three separate instances in which I, as a judge, have disqualified your entries for the same fault—a sagging back."

Mr. Gross had his own back against a wall, and he knew it. To continue such a discussion would only make him look increasingly foolish. He took a deep breath and decided to try another tack, but Miss Carstairs intercepted him.

"On my litter registration," she said, "which the A. K. C. holds in duplicate, I have a notation which should further serve to identify my dogs."

Mr. Gross looked up. "Yes?" He seemed on firmer ground again.

"Shadow and Sambo have no dewclaws," said Miss Amelia. "Dr. Clark, who attended the whelping and who also saw to the tail-cutting, can substantiate this."

Dr. Clark nodded, but Mr. Gross laughed. "That seems a very thin claim," he said. Then, feigning innocence, he asked, "Do the Matthews' pups have dewclaws?"

The vet whistled to Boy, and ran his hand up his forelegs. Then he picked the dog up and examined the legs more closely. There was complete silence as everyone waited. "This dog has no dewclaws. They've been removed," he said, "rather recently. The scar, while indistinct, is still visible."

Gross shrugged. "Perhaps you could find a scar on this other pup also, Dr. Clark." The words, "If it should be to your advantage," were unspoken but implied.

The vet's eyes narrowed, and he looked directly at Artemus Gross. "Miss Carstairs' two dogs were *born* without dewclaws," he said.

Mr. Gross knew when he was licked. He might have argued that it is no rare thing for dogs to be born without fifth toes, but he didn't. His face turned a pasty gray under the freckles, and he shrugged again. "Such a lot of commotion," he said, "over four black pups. I have thirty-two dogs in my kennels at present, all of them worth more attention than these. As far as I'm concerned, Miss Carstairs, you may have this dog"—he indicated Sambo—"and his brother too, if it will make you happy. I'll have my kennelman bring him down tonight." He rose and bowed.

But the pose he was assuming fooled no one. He was neither bored nor philanthropic; he was beaten to a standstill and yet trying to save face.

Miss Amelia, rather to the twins' disappointment, let him do so. She could afford to be gracious. "Mr. Matthews," she said, "will have the other two puppies ready to return with you to Gross Point."

But Mr. Gross waved his arm largely. "Keep them all," he shouted resonantly from the door. "Keep them all! I want no part of them." Without another word he strode hurriedly from the house.

The group in the living room stood quiet as the door slammed after him. Then Lynn turned timidly to Miss Amelia and spread her hands. "But *four* dogs," she said in genuine concern. "Daddy and I can never manage *four* dogs!"

Miss Amelia smiled down at her. "You won't have to, child," she said. "Shadow and Sambo are ready, now, to go back to Ohio with me." She cast a sidelong glance at Judy, who was standing, very tense and wide-eyed, listening. "As for Boy and Brother, if Mr. Gross won't take them back, I guess they're yours to dispose of as you see fit." She paused expectantly.

Lynn looked from Miss Carstairs to her father and must have read approval in his eyes. "I'd like Judy and Jeff to have one of them," she said, then added with an inflection that was unexpectedly childish, "if they're allowed."

Judy suddenly relaxed. She didn't realize how deeply she sighed or how bright her eyes became. "That would be wonderful, Lynn!" she cried. "I'm sure we'll be allowed."

Outside, as she finished speaking, the first big drops of rain began to fall.

Two days later Jeff lay full length on the diving board and stared down at the cool water. Behind him Boy, suddenly adventurous, scampered up and tickled the soles of his feet with his cold nose.

Judy, taking her turn with the small hand scythe at cutting down the grass which had grown tall by the edge of the pool during the drought, looked up when he yelled. "Look out, Boy!" she called. "You'll get a swimming lesson if you're not careful."

But the pup dodged Jeff's flailing legs expertly. He trotted back to land, then suddenly raised his nose, sniffing the summer air. Judy rested and watched him as he gave a short bark and started off, running into the wind. Halfway up the hill he met Brother, and the two pups frolicked back, tumbling over one another in reckless play. Behind them, more sedately, came Lynn, a blue sweater pulled over her bathing suit.

"Hi!" she called.

"Hi!" the twins called back.

"The water's swell!" Jeff added. Jumping to his

feet, he did a showy jackknife off the edge of the board.

He came to the surface quickly, to make sure that Lynn had watched him. "D'you think we should teach the puppies to swim?" he asked.

It was Judy who answered. "Not on your life," she said definitely. "I'm going to relax for the rest of the summer, now that the kidnaping's solved."

Jeff made a noise like a porpoise. "You can't exactly call it kidnaping," he said with mock seriousness. "How about dognaping?"

Judy howled and tore her hair. "That's awful!" she scolded. But the next minute her eyes were following the pups, who had discovered Jeff's old sweat shirt and were playing "tug of war," each with an arm in his teeth. "I'm glad of one thing," she said a minute later. "I'm glad Boy and Brother aren't show dogs. I'm glad they're just ordinary, run-of-the-mill cockers that nobody would want to steal."

"I'm glad they're *ours*," replied Lynn.